KU-242-405

COYOTE FALLS

Pat Calhoun rides into town and steps straight into the line of fire — and from that point onwards things get worse. Why has a gang of owlhoots gathered to cause trouble? Is there a connection to the Civil War and the man who betrayed him? Pat's only way of finding out is to ride straight into the outlaw nest . . . Events lead to an epic showdown, as Calhoun confronts his past, high above the raging Coyote Falls.

Books by Colin Bainbridge
in the Linford Western Library:

PACK RAT

COLIN BAINBRIDGE

COYOTE FALLS

Complete and Unabridged

LINFORD
Leicester

First published in Great Britain in 2011 by
Robert Hale Limited
London

First Linford Edition
published 2012
by arrangement with
Robert Hale Limited
London

The moral right of the author has been asserted

Copyright © 2010 by Colin Bainbridge
All rights reserved

British Library CIP Data

Bainbridge, Colin.
    Coyote Falls. - - (Linford western library)
    1. Western stories.
    2. Large type books.
    I. Title II. Series
    823.9'2–dc23

    ISBN 978–1–4448–1056–1

Published by
F. A. Thorpe (Publishing)
Anstey, Leicestershire

Set by Words & Graphics Ltd.
Anstey, Leicestershire
Printed and bound in Great Britain by
T. J. International Ltd., Padstow, Cornwall

This book is printed on acid-free paper

1

Straining against the wind and rain, Pat Calhoun leaned down from the saddle to read the name on the battered signpost: *Coyote Falls. No Gunfighters.* The finger pointed towards the sky but at least he knew he was on the right track. He had come a long way.

'Not far now, Cherokee,' he said.

There was a growl from the cougar.

'And remember to behave yourself in civilized company.'

He rode on, the cougar slinking along just ahead of him, riding point. Lightning began to flicker and he was carrying a rifle as well as his six-shooters. He had known of men who got burned for being caught that way and he thought about making camp. Thunder rolled down the sky. He carried on riding and as darkness fell he saw a few lights up ahead.

The rain-swept streets of town were

deserted. Light spilled from under the batwings of a saloon and a piano tinkled. He climbed from the leather, tied the dun to the hitch rack and entered the building with the cougar at his heels. Inside the air was thick with tobacco smoke. Cowboys sat around tables playing poker. Nobody seemed to notice the cougar until there was a sudden scream from a woman in a low-cut satin dress, standing by the bar. A few of the players looked up. The piano ceased in a minor key. A group of cowboys at the bar glanced slowly round and the bartender reached behind the counter.

'I wouldn't do that,' Calhoun said.

The woman screamed again and one of the cowboys reached for his gun. Calhoun's .44 was already in his hand.

'Just take it easy,' he said. 'The cat's tame. She won't hurt no one.'

The cowboy's hand remained suspended for a moment over his holster, then he slowly let it drop.

'What the hell?' somebody said.

'Go and get the marshal.'

The woman made for some stairs and ran up them two at a time. The men at the bar began to move aside. The batwings creaked as a few others took the opportunity to slip out.

'Better take it outside,' the barman said.

The cougar had seated itself at full length by a spittoon under the bar. Sawdust was sticking to its reddish-brown fur.

'She won't cause any bother. She's likely more worried about you than you are of her.'

A toothless oldster detached himself from a corner of the bar and approached the cat. Bending down, he stroked it behind the ear.

'Ain't never heard yet of a human bein' attacked by a cougar,' he said. 'Knowed a man kept a wolf as a pet. Now that's somethin' different.'

'You're right, old man,' Calhoun said. 'Here, let me buy you a drink.' He turned to the bartender. 'Whiskey for me an' my friend,' he said. 'Beer for the cat.'

The oldster's action seemed to have a calming effect. A few of the cowboys returned to the bar and the piano began to play again. The card games continued. Calhoun slipped his gun back into his belt and the bartender poured the whiskey. When he had finished he looked hesitantly at Calhoun.

'She'll take a glass,' Calhoun said, 'but a saucer would be better.' The old-timer took a long swig of the whiskey and Calhoun replenished his glass.

'Where'd you find her?' the old-timer asked.

'Got her from an Indian up on the Cherokee Strip. Weren't no more than a kitten. Brung her up myself.'

The old man looked reminiscent. 'The Cherokee Strip,' he mused. He glanced down at the horn-handled Army Colts tucked butt foremost into Calhoun's belt. 'One of the dangdest places I ever bin.' He held up his left hand from which the middle two fingers were missing.

'Left those behind in the Cherokee

Strip,' he said. 'Lucky to come away with the rest.'

Any further conversation was interrupted as the batwings swung open and the marshal appeared. He took a moment to glance around, then he saw the cougar. For just the fraction of a second he hesitated before striding to the bar.

'The cat belong to you?' he said to Calhoun.

Calhoun nodded.

'You read the sign outside o' town?'

'Sure. She ain't a gunfighter. Neither am I.'

'You shoulda checked those guns in with me.'

Calhoun glanced about the bar. Quite a few of the customers wore irons. 'What about them?' he said.

'That's different. They're regulars. And not too many of 'em are on friendly terms with a cougar.'

The oldster bent down and stroked the cat again. 'She ain't doin' no harm, Marshal,' he said. 'Just as friendly as a grass widder gatherin' her hay crop.'

Suddenly the batwings flew open again and three men burst into the room waving six-guns. The marshal looked up. Calhoun's Army Colt was already in his hand. As the men opened fire and the glass behind Calhoun's head shattered into fragments he pumped lead into one of the gunslingers. The marshal spun away as a bullet tore into his shoulder, and another man at the bar fell forwards, blood oozing from a jagged tear in his chest.

Calhoun fired again and another gunman went down. The third turned and began to run. At the same moment the cougar leaped forward. The man was part-way through the batwings when the cougar reached him, hurling herself forward and sinking her teeth into the man's gun arm. Down he went screaming as the cat began rending his flesh.

One of the gunmen Calhoun had shot struggled to his feet, firing wildly, but a slug from the marshal sent him spinning to the floor.

'Cherokee! Stop!' Calhoun called, and then: 'Ahiya'a!' He ran forward and pulled the cat away from the gunman's mangled arm. The cougar was growling and blood spattered her whiskers. The man was emitting a strange kind of sobbing sound as Calhoun dragged him to his feet. Apart from that, the bar was strangely quiet. People began to emerge from the shelter of tables and chairs. The marshal stepped forward, clutching at his shoulder, and clapped a pair of handcuffs around the gunslinger's wrists.

'Better get the doc!' someone shouted.

The bartender had come round from behind the bar and was examining the two gunmen who had been shot. 'Too late for these,' he said.

A few of the customers assisted him to drag the bodies outside. The oldster appeared with a bucket and mop and began to clear away the blood-soaked sawdust. Calhoun turned to the marshal.

'I'll be OK,' the marshal said. He was

losing quite a lot of blood but the wound was not serious. 'Let's take a walk,' he said to his prisoner.

He moved to the batwings and Calhoun went with him. Out in the street rain was still falling but the worst of the storm seemed to be over. They crossed to a small building which was the marshal's office and jail. By the time the gunman had been locked away the doctor arrived, carrying with him a worn black bag. He flinched when he saw the cougar but soon got about his business.

'This is going to hurt,' he said.

The marshal winced as the doctor prised out the bullet which had lodged beneath the collar bone.

'You were damn lucky this time,' the doctor said, bandaging up the wound.

When he had finished the marshal brought out a bottle of whiskey from a drawer in his desk and poured stiff measures all round.

'I guess I owe you,' he said to Calhoun.

'And Cherokee,' Calhoun replied.

The marshal laughed, grimacing with pain as he did so.

'I'd better check that varmint's arm,' the doctor said. While he was attending the injured man, Calhoun turned to the marshal.

'The doc said *this time*. What's this all about?'

'Ain't nothin' to concern you,' the marshal said.

'Maybe not. Who's to know till I hear the story.'

The marshal shrugged. 'First let me introduce myself. Name's Grayson, Jim Grayson.'

'Glad to make your acquaintance.'

'This used to be a quiet town. Just lately things have changed. There's been trouble. Some no-good owlhoots have been puttin' in an appearance. I had to shoot one of 'em. I figure there's a whole lot more makin' their home up in the hills. Used to be a mining camp up there, but it got abandoned a long time ago. I figure they're usin' it as some sort of retreat.'

Calhoun nodded. The doctor reappeared, but after turning down the offer of another drink, left the office.

'You take care,' he said to the marshal.

After he was gone there was a long silence. Eventually it was broken by Calhoun.

'I reckon you're right about those owlhoots,' he said.

The marshal looked up.

'Ever hear of a man named Johnny Carver?'

The marshal shook his head.

'No real reason you should. There's been a dodger out on him but not in this state. I knew him during the war. We were on the same side then. Leastways that's what I thought.'

'Is he somethin' to do with these owlhoots?'

'Can't be certain, but I have reason to believe he might be. Some people think the war's not over. Seems they never heard of Appomattox.'

'I've seen the type. Some of the boys

on both sides just don't seem able to settle down to normal life.'

'To cut a long story short, this *hombre* Carver betrayed me. More than that, he betrayed some friends of mine. I spent time in Andersonville because of him. I swore I'd get even. I reckon he's the man we're both lookin' for.'

The marshal downed the last of his whiskey. 'I could make you a deputy,' he said.

Calhoun shook his head. 'Thanks, but it ain't my style. Ain't you got no one else to back you up?'

'Deputy'll be by soon, but the town's runnin' scared. I can't blame 'em. They're peaceable folks. Never come up against nothin' like this before.'

'How far to this old minin' camp?' Calhoun asked.

'Hills is about fifteen miles out of town. Beyond them's the Big Beaver range. A man could get lost up there.'

Calhoun got to his feet. He peered out through the slats of the marshal's window.

'I'd best get movin',' he said. 'Make camp. Ain't no guest house likely to take ol' Cherokee.'

'No need to do that,' the marshal said. 'Like I say, I owe you. Why not stay over at my place?'

Calhoun looked at the cougar.

'I'm kinda gettin' used to her,' the marshal said. He paused for a moment. 'Ain't so sure about Mary, but I guess she might be persuaded.'

'Mary?'

'She's my sister. Since I came back to Coyote Falls after my wife died a couple o' years back I bin stayin' with her. The arrangement suits us both.'

Calhoun looked hesitant.

'She'd appreciate the company,' the marshal said. 'She runs a little eatin'-house off Main Street. The way she has to deal with some of her customers, that there cougar ain't gonna present no problem.'

*   *   *

When he was introduced to her, Calhoun was impressed with Mary in three ways. First of all she showed no fear of the cougar whatsoever. In the second place she was plumb pretty. In the third place she was an excellent cook.

'Thank you, ma'am,' Calhoun said when he had finished the last piece of apple pie. 'I ain't tasted anything like that in a long time.'

'You're very welcome,' she replied.

Calhoun turned to her brother. 'You're a lucky man.'

They sat out on the veranda to drink coffee. It was late. The rain had ceased and a pale moon came and went between scudding clouds. In an out-house Cherokee lay sleeping.

'I want to thank you for what you did for my brother,' Mary said.

Although she had shown obvious concern at the marshal's wounded shoulder, she had not previously mentioned the matter.

'It was nothin',' Calhoun replied.

'That's not true,' she said. 'If you hadn't have been there . . . ' She stopped short and Calhoun thought he detected the suggestion of a sob in her voice.

'Hey, how about that cougar,' Grayson remarked.

Mary rose to her feet. 'If you'll excuse me,' she said. 'I think I'll leave you boys to it.' After she had gone a hint of her perfume hung in the air.

'That's a mighty nice lady,' Calhoun said.

They sat back. Calhoun produced a pouch of Bull Durham and they both built smokes.

'Those owlhoots ain't gonna let this pass,' Grayson said eventually. 'That's three of 'em dead now and one in jail.'

'You're probably right. The townsfolk may be peaceable, but perhaps it's time you gave 'em a wake-up call.'

The marshal blew a ring of smoke into the night air. Tree leaves rattled in the wind.

'This *hombre* Carver. What's the story?'

14

Calhoun looked away. For a few moments he seemed to be wrestling with his memories before fixing his eyes on Grayson. Then he began to explain in almost unnecessary detail, as if he had to stick to a fixed narrative that he couldn't afford to vary.

He had been detailed to scout for the general commanding the division. His instructions were simple: get as near as possible to the enemy's lines and gather whatever information he could find. To get there he had to move through a densely wooded area, keeping off the beaten path in case remnants of the Rebels still remained. It was a dull day and dark beneath the boughs, and the undergrowth was dense. A lot of the time he could only make progress on his hands and knees. Moving forward with agonizing slowness he came to a narrow opening in the bushes through which he could see a mound of yellowish clay. It was a line of abandoned Confederate rifle pits but there were no signs of stragglers. There were no indications either of wounded soldiers. The place had simply been deserted. It was an important piece of news for the general.

He had come to an angle of the woods beyond which was the edge of a farm. It presented a forlorn and desolate sight, overgrown with weeds and brambles. The buildings were scorched and broken, with vacant apertures like unseeing eyes where the doors and windows had been smashed. It was obvious that no one had lived there for some time. Between Calhoun and the main building stretched an overgrown field and orchard: if he climbed one of the apple trees he would have a fine view over the surrounding countryside, from which he might be able to gain an idea of the enemy's disposition.

In this he was proved correct. The tree overlooked a long piece of open ground leading to a spur of the nearby mountain; a road across this was crowded with the Confederate rearguard, on the retreat, their gun-barrels gleaming in the sunlight. Now he had something to report.

For a moment he felt a huge sense of elation but his joy was cut short by a rushing sound which suddenly seemed to fill the air. It increased to a roar. Calhoun was confused, half expecting to see some huge bird come sweeping down upon him. It was no bird, however, and even as he realized what the sound was the missile struck with a deafening burst of noise, bringing down the tree and several others in a shattering explosion of dust and dirt, tree limbs and branches, and burying him in a pile of earth and debris.

He must have passed out. When he came round all he could see immediately in front of him was a high mound, which cut off his view of the trees in one direction. His head throbbed and there was a loud ringing in his ears. Dust was still billowing from the explosion. He became conscious of something running down the inside of his leg and when he tried to move a wave of pain instantly engulfed him. His left arm was twisted and caught behind him but he was able to move the right. He was in a bad situation. There was nothing he could do except hope that he might be discovered by Union troops advancing through the woods, but if ever they came it would probably be too late and they would find him dead. He was probably more dead than alive as it was.

He looked up at the sky. How blue he remembered it to have seemed, bluer than anything he had ever seen before, and very empty. He became aware of tears flowing down his cheeks but he could not understand why he was crying. Then another rush of pain swept through him like a crashing, surging billow and he was carried away into a dark submarine cave where there was no blue or any other colour.

Calhoun lit another cigarette. Although many nights had been lost in tormented dreams and nightmares it was not often that he thought consciously about those events. He had been lucky to come out alive and with nothing worse to show for it physically than a slight stiffness in the left arm and shoulder and the usual scars of battle. Even now he could not recall how he had managed to crawl to the shelter of the ruined farmhouse nor how long he had lain there, moving in and out of consciousness, before he had been found by refugees and nursed back to a semblance of health and the knowledge that he was behind enemy lines.

It was through the refugees that he was put in contact with Con Reeder. Con Reeder had been running an underground for some time, smuggling fugitives and Unionist sympathizers through the lines. He was assembling a small group to go over the mountains. Calhoun was too weak to make the first trip but he fought hard to make himself ready for the second.

Con Reeder was a shrewd man. He knew that no matter how remote and treacherous a route might be, there was no way to avoid leaving a trail. His method was to move rapidly, at breakneck pace, sometimes doubling back on himself or wading, neck deep, across icy streams.

It worked. When they began climbing Cumberland Mountain they were almost safe. The mountain provided good cover and on the other side they would come down into Kentucky. Calhoun recalled how the exhausted men began to relax and almost enjoy themselves at the prospects of safety: properly cooked food, home-made whiskey and a bed to sleep in. But they never made it down the mountain.

'The Confederates were waiting for us,' Calhoun concluded. 'They'd been tipped off. Carver was one of us, one of the group Reeder had put together, but I noticed at the time that he wasn't there when they opened fire. I think Reeder must have been killed straight off. A couple of us managed to run but it was no use. I was the only one to come out alive.'

Grayson had been listening intently.

He could see how much it cost his companion to recount the tale.

'This Carver has something to answer for,' he said. 'If you're right and he's up in those mountains somewhere, what do you intend doin' about it?'

Calhoun suddenly laughed. 'You know, I just ain't exactly sure.'

'You're ridin' up there?'

'Seems like it.'

'You're one man. What can you do against a whole nest of outlaws?'

'You're forgettin' Cherokee,' Calhoun replied.

★   ★   ★

The following day dawned bright and clear. Mary had arranged with Calhoun and her brother to eat breakfast at her café. She was looking just as pretty in a blue gingham dress and her dark hair was held back in a snood. The effect was to make her look a little older, and for the first time Calhoun noticed the beginnings of crow's feet at the corners of her eyes. He felt a sudden tenderness. The marshal's shoulder was feeling sore but otherwise he was OK.

'I hope you were comfortable last night,' Mary commented.

It was the first time for a long while that Calhoun had slept between sheets.

'I sure appreciate everything,' he said a little awkwardly.

The marshal laughed. 'Wait till you've tasted breakfast,' he said.

He wasn't exaggerating. Calhoun thought he had finished when he cleared his plate of eggs, bacon, steak, beans and hash browns. Then Mary reappeared with pancakes dripping with molasses and a fresh pot of strong black coffee. By that time a couple of townsfolk had come in and Mary was busy. Grayson glanced up at a clock on the back wall.

'Should be about time for the stage,' he said.

They got up and wandered down the street towards the stage depot. A little knot of people were gathered and inside the building the clerk was tying up a bag of letters. There was an air of expectancy, which grew as the minutes ticked by. A man in a dark suit and a fancy waistcoat pulled a watch out of his pocket and examined it. People were looking up for some sign of the stage's approach. Eventually the clerk came out and approached the marshal.

'She's late,' he said. 'I hope nothing's wrong.'

They waited a little longer and then the marshal turned to Calhoun.

'I got a feelin',' he said. 'Let's you an' me take a look.'

They moved over to the livery stable where Calhoun had left his horse. They saddled up, mounted their horses, turned down the runway and were soon out in open country. They rode at a steady lope for a while, following a clearly marked trail. The sun was getting hotter and black flies swarmed in the air. Grayson looked up and pointed.

'Buzzards,' he said.

Not long after that they came upon the coach, smashed and lying on its side. The bodies of the driver and guard were lying at a little distance. When they dismounted and looked inside they found three further corpses flung together; two men and a woman. There was no sign of the horses and the strongbox was missing together with the mail bag. Grayson bent over the bodies of the driver and the guard.

'Look here,' he said.

They had each been shot in the back of the head.

'Cold-blooded execution,' Calhoun snapped.

He went back to the coach and pulled at the door. It was jammed but after a considerable effort he succeeded in partly opening it. Between them Grayson and Calhoun dragged the bodies from the mangled wreckage.

'This is the third time something like this has happened,' Grayson said, 'but previously there were survivors. There's been nothin' as bad as this.'

'How much money was the stage carryin'?'

'I'd have to check with the clerk, but a substantial amount.'

'Those varmints must be gathering quite a store,' Calhoun said. 'Enough to fund somethin' big, if that's what they got in mind.'

'That's not all,' the marshal replied. 'There's rumours of treasure still left up there. Could be why they chose the place.'

There was nothing to be done for the moment except return to town and send the undertaker out with his wagon. Just as they were about to leave Calhoun noticed something lying on the grass. It was a sheet of white paper which had been attached to the door but had fallen to the ground. Bending down, he picked it up and unfolded it.

'What is it?' Grayson said.

Calhoun read out a message which had been scrawled across the paper:

The town next time.

They mounted their horses and began to ride.

'What do you think?' the marshal said.

'I think they mean it,' Calhoun replied. 'I guess we'd better treat it that way.'

A thought came into Calhoun's head. 'What's the last town the stage would've stopped before this?'

'Lone Gulch. There's a relay station halfway between. Why do you ask?'

Before Calhoun could reply there came a flash of light followed by the reverberating roar of a rifle. Grayson's horse went down, flinging its rider to the ground. At the same instant Calhoun slid from the saddle, dragging his horse down in the same movement so that it lay flat beside the marshal's wounded bay. Sheltering behind them, they drew their guns, searching the terrain for their attacker.

'See anything?' Grayson snapped. The wound to his shoulder had started to bleed again and his mouth was drawn tight with pain.

There was plenty of cover nearby, enough to conceal several bushwhackers if they'd known what they were doing. But the fact that the shot hadn't hit either of them suggested to Calhoun that they weren't up against a professional. And he hadn't seen any signs of hoofprints along the trail.

'Wait,' he said. 'He'll give himself away.'

Seconds later there was a stab of flame from a patch of bushes and a shot whined nearby, kicking up dirt. Instantly Calhoun's gun barked in reply.

'Cover me,' Calhoun said.

In a flash he was on his feet and running zigzag towards the bushes. Grayson's gun beat a fusillade behind him and as he got closer he opened fire at the screen of vegetation. There was an answering shot and then movement as someone hidden behind the bushes got to his feet and began to run, flinging his rifle away as he did so. Calhoun held his fire and swerved away in hot pursuit.

Could do with Cherokee right now, he thought.

The man was no match for him, however, and as Calhoun steadily gained ground the man suddenly stopped and turned to meet his pursuer, his hands held high in the air.

'Don't shoot! Don't shoot!' he screamed.

Not taking any chances, Calhoun threw himself upon the man and carried him to the ground. The man gasped as air was driven from his body. Calhoun got to his feet and stood over him with his gun.

'Grayson!' he called. 'I've got him!'

By the time the marshal arrived the man had recovered a little and he was staring up at them with a puzzled expression on his features. Calhoun's face bore a similar look. The man didn't look like any kind of outlaw. He was very young, fresh-faced and clean-shaven and he wore a set of fancy duds which looked out of place.

'You ain't the outlaws!' he gasped.

'I was about to say the same,' Calhoun replied.

The man struggled to his feet and then he saw the marshal's badge.

'By Jiminy,' he said. 'Am I glad to see you.'

'You'd better have a good story,' Grayson snapped. 'You shot my horse. Lucky for you he ain't hurt too bad.'

'I was on the stage,' the youngster began. 'I was firing at the varmints who attacked us when the door flew open and I fell out. I thought you were the outlaws.' He paused as though he had run out of steam. He visibly sagged.

'What happened to the others?' he said.

The marshal shook his head.

'There was nothin' we could do,' Calhoun added.

'That was a real nice lady,' the man mused.

'Reckon we'd best get on back to town,' Calhoun said. He turned to the marshal. 'Your hoss up to carryin' you?'

'Like I say, he ain't hurt bad.'

'You can ride with me,' Calhoun said to the new-comer. As they walked the young man introduced himself as Hiram Jasper Bingley.

'That's some name,' Grayson said.

'What you doin' in these parts?'

'Just qualified from law school. Everybody seemed to think there'd be a need for lawyers out West.'

'Like a wool shirt in cow country,' Calhoun remarked.

'I just can't believe it,' Bingley said. 'My first stage-coach ride.'

'Coyote Falls is a long way from anywhere. It ain't much of a burg.'

'My uncle runs the Crutch Bar spread. I'm stayin' with him till I can fix myself up in town.'

Grayson stopped momentarily. 'So old Jake Adams is your uncle! Well I'll be danged.'

'On my mother's side,' Bingley said.

When they reached town they left the horses at the livery stable. Bingley's bullet had scorched the bay's flank but it was nothing the ostler couldn't handle.

Grayson rousted out the undertaker; soon his wagon was trundling its way along the street. There was no sign of Bingley's uncle at the stage depot.

'Guess you could do with some feedin',' Grayson commented. They made their way to Mary's café but it was closed. Grayson looked unsurprised. 'Guess you'd best come on back with us.'

When they arrived at the house it was to find Mary in the outhouse bending over the cougar, which she had just fed.

'I thought she might appreciate a bit of home cooking,' she remarked. The expression on Bingley's face was priceless.

'They make everythin' bigger out West,' Calhoun said. 'She ain't nothin' but a pussy cat.'

2

For a few days there was quiet. Hiram Bingley had left for his uncle's ranch. The doctor had been out to check on the marshal but his wounded shoulder was well on the way to recovery. Things were busy at Mary's café and Calhoun would have left but for the message on the piece of paper and the fact that the marshal asked him to stay on.

'I gotta feelin' things are goin' to blow apart real soon,' Grayson said.

Truth was that Calhoun felt the same. 'At least let me move out of the house,' he said. 'Mary must have plenty on her plate without me.'

'Nonsense,' Grayson replied. 'In fact, you just try it and see her reaction.'

Calhoun wasn't sure but he put off making a decision. At least while he stayed where he was the cougar didn't present a problem.

The marshal called a meeting to put the situation to the townsfolk. He didn't mention the message he and Calhoun had found because he didn't want to cause a panic, but on the other hand both he and Calhoun felt that the time had come to take some precautionary measures. The meeting was not well attended but the results, if patchy, were soon in evidence as up and down the main street storekeepers began to board up their windows. At either end of the drag, at the approaches to town, carts and wagons were positioned so as to be ready to form barricades if they were needed. Nobody was too sure, though, of what to expect and some people openly ridiculed any suggestion that such measures might be necessary. Mary was particularly concerned because she realized that if it came to fighting her brother would be in the forefront and she was more grateful than ever that Calhoun was around. People were jumpy and Calhoun decided to take a ride to see if he could find anything more definite.

He rode out towards the Crutch Bar but before he was even near the place he could see that something was afoot. All along the boundary line fences were in process of being erected and already a considerable amount of open range had been enclosed. Posts had been placed at thirty-foot intervals and men were working with fence stretchers to bind the wire tight to the posts. Riding down the line he came upon a wagon stretching wire as it rolled.

'Expectin' trouble?' he asked.

The foreman looked up. 'Ain't you the *hombre* with the cat?' he said.

'Hey, the one shot up those owlhoots in the saloon?' another man said. 'Man, that was some shootin'.'

Calhoun nodded. 'Had no choice.'

'Some cattle been disappearin',' the foreman said. 'Figure it's the same varmints.' He bent down to fasten some wire to a boulder for extra support. 'For what it's worth,' he said, 'A couple of the boys was out brush-poppin'. They seen a lot of riders gatherin' in the foothills.'

'Thanks,' Calhoun replied. 'Figure I might take a look that way.' He turned his horse. 'Give my regards to Hiram Bingley,' he added over his shoulder.

The foreman looked puzzled as he rode away. It didn't take him long to verify what the foreman had said. There was plenty of sign indicating that horsemen had been passing through. Topping a ridge, but being careful to avoid being skylined, he took a look through his field glasses. A big group of riders was camped beside a stream and they weren't there for a revival meeting.

Things moved rapidly and back in Coyote Falls the townsfolk were as ready as they were ever going to be. From his vantage point on the roof of the Silver Star saloon Calhoun took stock of the situation. Most of the buildings in the main street had now been boarded up and wagons swung into position to blockade it at either end. At strategic intervals along the street and on the rooftops men were placed, volunteers who had some idea of how to use a gun. The streets themselves were deserted; all the women and children and those who for one reason or another were not fit or able to take part in the anticipated fighting having taken shelter in houses situated away from the main drag. Even so Calhoun felt some anxiety about Mary.

He checked his Army revolvers and Henry rifle, the rifle he had carried through the Civil War, and jacked shells into a new Winchester Model 1866. A nice weapon but relatively untried. Then he turned his attention to the trail leading out of town. He could see nothing untoward but suddenly his ears seemed to catch the distant sound of horses. The sounds died away and, listen as carefully as he might, Calhoun heard no more. He found that his throat was dry and he took a swig of water from a canteen.

There was something strange and unnatural about things. Time seemed suspended and an air of expectancy enveloped the town. The atmosphere was oppressive and on the western horizon dark clouds hung over the landscape. A flicker of lightning danced along the edge of the sky. Maybe it had been the distant storm that he had heard. A wind had developed, blowing clumps of tumbleweed along the empty street. A few window frames rattled and a dog began to bark. He took another swig from the canteen. Something soporific in the atmosphere made him feel heavy-headed and then he heard someone shout:

'I think they're coming!'

Instantly alert, he looked up and after a moment saw what the man had seen; a faint haze of dust which slowly resolved itself into a host of riders, bearing down on the waiting town. Calhoun glanced down at the barricade across the street below. A line of men with rifles was stationed behind it, prominent among them being Marshal Grayson.

The riders came on and Calhoun

reckoned there were probably a dozen or more of them. Looking the other way, he saw another group of riders coming from the opposite direction. The outlaws had obviously divided their forces in order to hit the town on two fronts.

The nearer group slowed and came to a halt. The riders had seen the barricade drawn across the street. For a moment they hesitated but then they came on again. Calhoun had hoped they might stop to parley with the marshal. In the war the cavalry had been vital in getting from one place to another quickly, but they usually dismounted in order to fight. Not this bunch. Instead they fanned out but kept right on coming.

He raised his rifle as a fusillade of shots rang out from the approaching horsemen. At a signal from the marshal the men behind the barricades began to reply in kind and the whole place exploded in a crescendo of noise. Calhoun squeezed the trigger of his

Winchester but in the uproar that now prevailed he could not tell whether his shot had been successful. A number of the charging horses were down but it made no difference to the impetus of the onslaught. Like a great curving wave the horsemen bore down on the barricade as its defenders fired off another round of bullets and then began to break for the shelter of the buildings in its rear.

Only the marshal and a few others remained as the wave of attackers finally burst upon the barricade. Calhoun was firing rapidly and now a fresh rain of fire exploded from behind the shutters of the buildings. A couple of horses went down in the street. Other horses were entangled in the barricade and men were firing pistols at close range.

Looking up over the rooftops, Calhoun could see horsemen entering the town by some of the side streets, and back along the main drag a fierce encounter was taking place at the other barricade. The defenders were putting up a good fight but it seemed there just weren't enough of them.

Calhoun had time to see the marshal racing for cover behind an overturned wagon before he leaped to his feet and ran to the end of the rooftop. He jumped over the parapet to land on the roof of the building next to it. He was firing as he went and now bullets were screaming through the air and passing menacingly close overhead. Coming to the opposite end of the roof he lowered himself over the edge to drop the rest of the way into an alley below. Then he ran to the end of the alley and began to pour lead at the horsemen who were now galloping down the street in numbers. He wanted to get among the streets and alleys on the far side in an attempt to counter the riders who had circled round. It was also the side of town on which Mary's café was situated.

Choosing a moment when the street seemed relatively free of combatants he ran out into the open, crouched and still firing as he went. A rider suddenly appeared as if from nowhere, bearing down on him, but he rolled out of the way of the horse's hoofs and fired upwards at the rider who flung up his arms and went flying backwards out of the saddle. He lay inert in the dust of the road while the horse continued to hurtle wide-eyed down the main street.

Calhoun was in danger now of being shot at by his own side as well as the enemy. Out of the corner of his eye he saw the marshal sprinting for the saloon where he crashed through the batwings to take up another position from which to spray lead into the attackers who had at last overcome the barriers at either end of the street.

Calhoun was exposed but he picked himself up and made a dash for a corner of another alley. He made it as a hail of bullets tore up the dirt around his feet. He had already discarded the Henry on the roof of the building and now the Winchester was hot in his hands. Running out of ammunition he threw it aside and drew his Army Colts. Looking down the alley he could see horsemen passing across the entrance.

He had began to move down the alley when his attention was attracted by a dark pall of smoke which began to swirl across the lower end of the main street. He realized that one of the buildings had been set on fire. Smoke continued to billow, then a column of flame burst through the roof of one of the stores accompanied by the sibilant crackling of fire.

For a moment he considered trying to battle his way down the main drag towards the fire but, thinking better of it, he continued down the narrow passage between two high buildings which led to a parallel street of smaller stores and frame houses.

Reaching the end he poked his head out to ascertain what was happening. A couple of riders were coming towards him. He stepped out into the open, fanning the hammer of his gun, and both riders toppled from the saddle. The spurs of one of the riders became entangled in the stirrups as the frightened horse set off at a wild gallop, dragging the man along with it. His screams rang in Calhoun's ears as he ran along the street in the direction of the fire.

Dense clouds of smoke were now pouring from the burning building and as fresh flowers of flame began to bloom above the rooftops it was obvious that other buildings had caught alight. The sounds of gunfire were being drowned by the crackle and roar of the flames.

Veering off down another turning, he emerged on to the main street again. Even as he sprinted for cover there came a shattering explosion and the saloon in which Grayson had sought shelter ripped apart. A dazzling sheet of fire swept across the road burning and singeing Calhoun with its heat and causing him to be momentarily disorientated by the blast. His ears rang and there was blood coming out of his nose, but shaking his head to get rid of the concussion, he ran forward again, bursting through the batwing doors.

'Grayson!' he screamed. 'Are you in there?'

The saloon was a mass of flame and dense black smoke and the stairs had been partly blown away. There was no response to his shouted question but through the dense pall of smoke Calhoun detected the shape of a body lying sprawled across the stairs on the top landing. Tying his kerchief over his mouth and keeping his eyes partly closed against the stinging effect of the smoke he managed to make it to the foot of the stairs. Further progress seemed impossible, however, as there was only a yawning gap where the middle section of the stairwell should have been.

'Grayson!' he shouted again. 'Can you hear me?'

The figure at the top of the stairs suddenly stirred and, coughing and spluttering, the marshal struggled to his knees and began to crawl forwards.

'Is that you, Calhoun?' he managed to gasp.

'Yes, it's Calhoun. Try and get as far

as you can down the stairs and then jump.'

The marshal coughed again, then seemed to gather his wits. Getting to his feet he staggered down the few remaining stairs, clinging to the wall. When he reached the last remaining stair he stood looking about. The heat was overwhelming and Calhoun realized that there could be further explosions at any moment. He was blinded by the smoke and his throat and lungs were burning.

'Jump!' he repeated.

In the next instant the marshal had launched himself off the stair to come crashing down on the floor beneath, toppling over and wincing with pain. Calhoun made his way to the marshal's side.

'I've done my ankle,' Grayson said.

Without bothering to reply Calhoun bent down and hauled the marshal to his feet, holding him beneath one armpit and putting the marshal's other arm over his shoulder.

He stepped forward and the marshal gasped with pain.

'Sorry,' Calhoun said, 'but we've got to get out of here.'

Somewhere at the back of the saloon there came another loud bang and what was left of the bar came crashing forwards, sending splinters and slivers of glass flying through the air. Gasping for breath the two men inched forwards towards the door, having to take a detour to avoid huge tongues of flame which barred a more direct route to the exit. To Calhoun the going seemed infinitely slow and the marshal was a dead weight but somehow they managed to reach the batwings and stagger outside. The marshal hopped a few more paces before they both collapsed to the ground in the shelter of a water trough.

Calhoun took off his bandanna, soaked it in the water and held it first to the marshal's face and then to his own. His skin was blistered and burnt but the cold water brought a blessed sense of relief. Struggling to turn his head he observed what was happening in the street. Gunfire was still booming and there seemed to be something going on at the opposite end of the drag to where the fires were raging. A group of riders had dismounted and were throwing burning faggots into the buildings and on to the roofs. Flames began to spread from that end of town also. In between there were bodies of men and horses lying in the dust which swirled around thick with the smell of ash and smoke.

'Isn't the café thataway?' the marshal spluttered. 'Better get down there.'

Calhoun hesitated. 'What about you?' he asked.

'I'll be all right,' the marshal said. Calhoun looked at him. The marshal's hair and eyebrows were singed and his face was black. His clothes hung in tattered rags around him and he could barely move because of his injured ankle. Despite everything and for no reason Calhoun couldn't help grinning.

'Sure, you'll be fine,' he said and,

seeing that the marshal had lost his weapons, he thrust one of his Colts into his hand.

'Take this,' he said. 'Stay here under cover of the horse trough.'

'Guess I ain't got much option,' the marshal said.

Things seemed quiet temporarily and Calhoun took advantage of it to dart across the road and back down the alley. Sheets of flame were billowing over the intervening roofs and a pall of smoke hung in the air. Sounds of shooting still burst upon his ears from the direction of the main street but it was becoming more sporadic. After all the fury and pandemonium this area seemed eerily calm.

As he arrived at a familiar junction Calhoun could see Mary's eating-house up ahead. Mercifully it was untouched by the flames and, although he knew she was not in there anyway, he felt a sense of relief. He turned and started down the street. Black smoke was billowing everywhere but the sounds of shooting seemed to have subsided.

Suddenly a figure loomed into view from behind a tree, taking Calhoun by surprise. A gun exploded in the man's hand and Calhoun felt a sharp pain in his right shoulder as a bullet scorched his flesh. The next bullet might have found its mark but just as the man pointed it again, pausing for a second to steady his aim, a brown blur flashed across the space between them. It was Cherokee, the cougar. The man let out a gasp of pain as the cougar's teeth buried themselves in his hand. Then Calhoun's gun spat flame and lead and the man was lifted backwards by the impact of the slug. He fell to the ground in a welter of blood, the cougar still clinging to his hand. Calhoun prepared to fire again but the man did not move and when Calhoun came up it was clear that he was dead.

'It's OK, girl,' Calhoun said. 'Ahiya'a!' The cougar seemed reluctant to release its grip of the man's hand but as Calhoun bent down to stroke her she ceased growling. 'Where did you come from?' Calhoun said.

It was not the first time that kind of thing had happened. He guessed that the animal, excited by all the noise and shooting, had escaped from the outhouse. As he kneeled drops of rain began to splatter from the overcast sky. The storm which he had observed on the horizon from the rooftop had arrived over the town.

Calhoun began to run back the way he had come, the cougar running alongside him. When he turned into the main street buildings were still burning at either end but already the flames were less rampant as the driving rain began to quench them. There was no further fighting taking place and no sign either of the riders. Only dead men and horses littered the street.

A group of men were continuing to fight the fire and it looked as though the storm might have spared the rest of the town. Gun in hand in case of further eventualities, Calhoun ran down the street in search of the marshal whom he had left behind the water trough.

He was still there, stretched out in exhaustion and scarcely able to move even if he had wanted to. Behind him the saloon was a smouldering shell. Flames were still licking quite high but the rain would soon extinguish them. A powerful acrid smell filled the air.

'We done it!' Grayson said. 'We beat them off!' Calhoun took the marshal in his arms, carried him to his office and laid him on a bunk in the corner. 'I'll get the doc,' he said.

'Leave it!' Grayson snapped. 'There must be others needing his help more than me.'

'Are you sure you'll be OK?'

Just at that moment the door flew open and Mary ran in. 'I couldn't sit and wait any longer,' she gasped.

Calhoun hesitated a moment more.

'I'll see to him,' Mary said. Turning to Calhoun with an appeal in her eyes, she added: 'Please be careful.'

Carrying that look with him, Calhoun rushed out and ran down the street to join the small group of townsmen who had been fighting the larger fires at the other end of town. There wasn't a lot to be done except help the rain by pouring buckets of water over the lingering flames and over the smouldering ruins to prevent them catching fire again. A few people were beating at the flames with blankets.

Presently they were joined by more helpers as people began to emerge from shelter. The undertaker's wagon appeared rolling down the street, collecting bodies.

It was a scene of misery and desolation. A number of the buildings along the main street at this end were completely destroyed and others were badly damaged. A pall of smoke and ash hung over the town and always the driving rain came battering down as though the heavens wept. Corpses of men and horses still littered the roadway and the only movement was the undertaker's cart.

Calhoun carried on walking. At the

opposite end of town there was a similar scene of destroyed and damaged buildings and debris from the barricade littered the ground. Calhoun felt utterly weary. He did not know how many people had been killed on either side or whether the battle was truly over. Maybe the remaining attackers would come back again to finish the job. For the present he did not care.

Feeling numb with tiredness, wet through and hurting from his various wounds, he began to stagger down the street towards where he had left the marshal and Mary.

3

Hiram Bingley awoke on the day following his arrival at the Crutch Bar feeling little the worse for his encounter with the outlaws. After eating a hearty breakfast he wandered out into the yard. A few cowboys were just coming out of the bunkhouse and a couple of others were slouching around the corral rails.

'Mornin'!' one of them called, an old hand named Orne Thompson. Hiram lifted his hat and walked over to join them.

'Mighty fine day,' Thompson said.

'Sure is.'

'Doin' anythin' much?'

'Nope.'

Thompson spat and looked at his fellows. 'Thing is,' he said, 'me an' the boys were just figurin' to fix up a little badger fight. Wondered if you might be interested.'

Bingley nodded. There was an eager if puzzled look on his face. Thompson indicated a big burly cowboy who was sitting on a fence rail.

'Ray here reckons he has the most fierce ornery damn badger in the territory. Isn't that so?'

The big man spat. 'Ain't no dog can beat her,' he said.

There were some shouts from the cowboys. Thompson smiled and held up his hand to restore order.

'We'll see. Thing is, most of the boys have got their money on either the dog or the badger. We need someone to be referee. Someone without any pecun'ary int'rest, if you see what I mean.'

'You mean you want me to be referee? Goldurn it, I'd be plumb honoured.'

Quite a big crowd of cowpokes had now joined the group at the corral and with one accord they began to move towards some outhouses. As they went they were whooping and shouting and a degree of excitement was in the air.

'What do I have to do?' Bingley enquired.

'Don't worry none. There ain't nothin' to it,' Thompson said, proceeding to give Bingley some basic advice on how to hold the badger. 'Pull hard an' you'll be helpin' the dog, pull soft an' you'll be favourin' the badger.'

Bingley nodded but was beginning to feel a little apprehensive. The whole group came round the side of a barn; tethered to a post at a corner of an open space was a bedraggled dog.

'There he is,' the big man called Ray said. 'Ain't he a beaut?'

Bingley looked at the dog. It was lying full length and had apparently just woken from its sleep. It raised a bloodshot eye and looked at Bingley. Both of them wore a similar expression on their faces.

'He don't look like a fighter,' Bingley exclaimed after a few moments. In fact the dog looked like a mangy cur. Nearby was a large tub with a length of rope running out some distance into the yard.

'The badger's under there,' Thompson said.

'Here, let me explain the rules,' someone added. He stepped out and began
to explain to Bingley what he had to do.

'When Thompson gives the order to
pull, just give the rope a good hard
yank,' he concluded.

Ray bent down and untied the dog.
For a few moments it remained inert
before slowly struggling to its feet and
shaking.

'Thataboy Rocky,' Ray said.

The group had gathered in a circle
about Bingley. Bingley looked round at
them expectantly. His hands gripped
the rope tightly and his arms were taut.

'Pull!' yelled Thompson.

Bingley pulled the rope. At the same
moment a cowboy tipped the tub from
the rear. Over Bingley went in the dust
to howls of laughter from the watchers
and where he had expected the badger
to be hidden was a chamber-pot full of
stale beer.

'Watch out for the hell-hound!' someone
shouted.

'My money's on the badger!' came

the reply. The laughter continued as Bingley dragged himself to his feet.

'Good job he got some dirt on that there shirt. The glare was beginnin' to hurt my eyes.'

'Won't need no mail-order catalogue. We got a livin' one right here.'

Bingley gave an embarrassed grin.

'Come on,' Thompson said, slapping him on the back. 'Let's head for the bunkhouse. I reckon you could do with a real drink.'

Laughing and joking they came round the corner of the corral. Bingley's uncle was standing on the veranda with a broad grin on his face.

'Don't be too hard on him, boys!' he shouted. 'Or I'll have my sister to answer to!'

* * *

Back in town there was concern that the riders would return, but there was no sign of them by evening and people began to feel a little easier. By that time a clearer picture of what had occurred had begun to emerge. The townsfolk had lost five of their number and in addition there were twice as many carrying injuries, at least two of which were relatively serious. Still, the doctor expected them to make a full recovery. One of the minor wounded was the marshal.

Of the attackers nine had been killed. There was no way of calculating how many had been wounded because if there were any they had managed to get away. Only one slightly wounded man had been caught and he was recuperating in the town jail along with the gunslick the marshal had arrested previously.

The town was a mess but already steps had been taken to begin clearing away the wreckage. It was the storm that had saved it from an even worse fate. All the rest of that day the rain had poured down, only beginning to clear as darkness fell.

Late in the evening Calhoun called to

see how the marshal was doing. He had been moved to his own house and was sitting up with his bandaged foot on a stool. Mary gave Calhoun an exasperated look.

'Stubborn!!' was the only word she used but that was enough.

'Damned foot,' Grayson said as Calhoun took a seat beside him. 'Doc reckons it could take a while before I can get around properly again.' He pointed to a crutch leaning up against the wall.

'I insisted on that,' he said. 'At least I can stagger about that way. Better than bein' laid up completely.'

'You take it steady,' Calhoun said. 'No point in makin' things worse.'

There was a box of cigars lying on a nearby table and the marshal offered one to Calhoun. They both lit up and began to puff away. A large glass of whiskey added to the enjoyment.

'Reckon those varmints got taught a lesson,' the marshal said.

'Guess so. Leastways, I don't figure

they'll be back for more, not for a while.'

'Bit off more than they could chew. And they'll know we'll be even more ready for 'em if they did decide to try again.' The marshal paused to drink his whiskey as Mary rejoined them.

'All the same,' she said, 'they seemed to go to an awful lot of trouble.'

They all pondered her words.

'They're scum,' Calhoun said. 'If I'm right about them they've got so used to doin' whatever they liked in the war they think they can go right on as if nothin's changed.'

'Was some trouble hereabouts,' the marshal added. 'Back in '63. Some Rebs got themselves hanged. Maybe they was takin' time out to settle a few old scores.'

Calhoun was thoughtful. 'You could be right,' he said.

They had finished their drinks and their cigars. 'Think I'll be turnin' in,' the marshal said. 'How about you, Calhoun?'

'Yeah, pretty soon. But I think I might just take a stroll down town, see how things are first.' He got to his feet and made to step off the porch when Mary spoke.

'Mind if I come with you? I guess all these events have made me unsettled.'

Calhoun felt a strange flush of excitement. 'I'd be honoured ma'am,' he replied.

'Are you sure you can manage on your own with those crutches?' Mary said.

'Just git movin' before I throw 'em at you,' her brother replied.

Together Calhoun and Mary stepped down off the veranda, and when they had closed the gate in the wicket fence behind them she took Calhoun's arm. It seemed natural. Without feeling any need for words they walked through the outlying streets towards the centre of town. The rain had ceased and only scattered remnants of clouds blew about the sky.

Coming at length to the burned-out

saloon, they stood and looked closely at the shattered pile of debris. The front was completely blown out and in the darkness at the back they could see the broken staircase hanging crazily in the air. The marshal had been lucky to survive the blast at all. A damaged ankle and some minor burns seemed a small price to pay for having been in the building when it blew apart.

'Almost looks like the place has been abandoned,' Calhoun remarked.

The streets were deserted. Traces of blood still remained in the dust like the spilled gore of the buildings themselves. Their walls were pockmarked with bullets and great gaping holes like sightless eyes stared blindly out where windows had been shattered. Broken shutters hung at crazy angles and swung creaking in the breeze. Mary seemed to take a firmer hold of his arm.

'My brother would never have come out alive if it wasn't for you,' she remarked. 'This is the second time I've had to thank you.'

He looked down at her. Her eyes were gleaming and filled with unshed tears. He felt an urge to take her in his arms but instead they carried on walking, moving out into the centre of the street. A gibbous moon swung out from behind some clouds and hung above the roofs of the still smouldering buildings.

'You're going after them, aren't you,' she said suddenly.

Calhoun was taken unawares.

'My brother has said something — about a man named Carver.'

Calhoun would have preferred the conversation not to have taken the turn it had, but there was no way now he could avoid it.

'That was my intention from the start,' he said. 'What has happened here has only convinced me even more that the man I want is up in the hills somewhere.'

'And you think he's the man behind what happened here?'

Calhoun nodded. 'What do you know about a mining camp in the hills?' he

64

asked. 'Your brother seems to think there was silver up there.'

'So some people say,' she remarked. 'There was even a small town. I believe they called it Elk Creek.' They turned and began to retrace their steps. 'Do you really have to go?' she said.

Calhoun was silent. As they approached the house he looked down at her.

'I have to go,' he said. 'But I aim to come back.'

The boys from the Crutch Bar were setting off on a snipe hunt, bringing with them a chastened Hiram Bingley. He was wearing a different set of duds, having been persuaded by his uncle, Jake Adams, that the outfit he had chosen really wasn't the most appropriate for helping round the ranch. Hiram had expressed an interest in staying around for a few days before checking out what property might be available in town in which to set up his law practice.

'That's good,' Adams said. 'You took that bit o' nonsense from the boys this mornin' real well. They're a good crew.

Don't take it to heart if they josh you around a bit.'

Orne Thompson had suggested that Bingley should come along with them. Ray Cole and a few of the others from the morning's activities were there. Bingley was riding a big skewbald. He could ride well enough but his uncle had thought it wise to choose a horse for him and had checked it personally for any sign of burrs under the saddle blanket.

'We bin plannin' this for a whiles,' Thompson said. If Bingley had any doubts, he did not show them.

'Ain't nothin' to beat snipe for taste,' Cole remarked. 'An' just as easy to catch as all get-out.'

'Can't say as I've tasted it,' Bingley remarked. 'Kinda like turkey at Thanksgiving, is it?'

'Yup, you got it.'

'Flapjacks with maple syrup to follow.'

They were riding towards the foothills. It was a clear evening with stars just beginning to glimmer and gleam. They splashed through a narrow stream overhung by cottonwoods and willows.

'Ain't I seen this before?' Bingley commented. 'Looks kind of familiar.'

'Lotta creeks. They look pretty much the same.'

'Seems like we bin through this swampy patch already.'

'Like I say, that's just the way it is.'

They rode a little further and then Thompson drew them to a halt.

'Right about here should do it,' he said.

They dismounted and a couple of the cowboys lit a lantern.

'Here, take this,' Thompson said. He handed Bingley a gunny sack.

'Now remember what you gotta do,' Cole said. 'The main thing is to keep the mouth of the sack wide open. The light will attract the snipe right into the sack so long as you keep it open.'

'I understand,' Bingley said.

Thompson was giving a demonstration of how to squat down and hold the sack. 'You sure about it?' he said.

'Seems easy enough,' Bingley replied.

'OK. The rest of us will just mount up and go drive in the snipe. We got a heap o' country to cover.'

'Don't forget to take his hoss,' Cole added. 'Otherwise that pinto is just set to scare the snipe away.'

With a final few words of advice they rode off. Bingley watched them go and when the last thuds of their hoofbeats had died away he turned to the task in hand. He didn't know how long it would take them to drive in the snipe but he was prepared for a decent wait. It was a pity, though, that there were so many black flies and mosquitoes about. They seemed to be drawn by the lantern. It wasn't going to be any picnic but he was determined to show them what a good snipe hunter he would make. They would sure appreciate snipe on the menu back at the Crutch Bar.

It got dark and after he had been waiting a long time he began to wonder why there were still no signs of snipe.

Thompson had advised him that it might take a good time; maybe they were just an elusive kind of bird. His back began to ache and reluctantly he dropped the gunny sack. He began to doze.

When he awoke the sky was ablaze with constellations. He had no way of telling the time but he had a feeling that it was long past midnight. His limbs were aching a little and he felt cramped. Flies were still making a nuisance of themselves and he was itching from their bites. Getting to his feet, he began to stamp up and down till he felt better. Glancing down, he saw the gunny sack and bent down to peer inside in case some of the snipe had somehow found their way in. It was empty so he resumed his earlier position and squatted down, holding open the mouth of the sack.

It was only after he had been waiting that way for a long time that he began to feel suspicious. He remembered the badger fight. The first signs of dawn were paling the horizon when at last he decided that he had been jobbed for a second time.

'Goldurn those danged cowpokes,' he said to himself. 'Looks like there's only one snipe around here and it's me.'

Apart from his aches and pains he was beginning to feel decidedly hungry. They had left him with some water in a canteen and a few strips of jerky and he started on them.

'Keep me goin' till I hit town,' he said.

When he had finished he got to his feet and looked around for the pinto. It was only then that he recalled they had taken his horse with them.

'Damnit,' he said. 'Now I'm stuck. Must be a good long ways back to Coyote Falls.'

He was talking because he was feeling lonely. Dawn was washing out the stars and a cool wind was blowing from the distant hills. A bird began to call. Suddenly he felt nervous. He looked around him. The trees and bushes seemed to be watching him and the shadows concealed a hidden and mysterious life of their own. He thought he heard something and his attention was drawn to a patch of vegetation by a suggestion of movement. Maybe he was wrong. Maybe it was just the flickering of the leaves.

He was about to start walking when the bushes abruptly parted and a cougar stepped into view. Bingley's blood ran cold and he was so frozen with fear that he forgot the six-gun he had in his belt. His mouth opened but no sound came from it. The cougar looked at him, its head slightly cocked to one side, and then it opened its mouth in turn and let out a fearsome roar which rang in Bingley's ears like a knell of doom. He had just enough presence of mind to begin edging slowly away although his legs scarcely obeyed him and his knees were trembling. The cougar began to creep forwards.

Sweat had sprung out on Bingley's

brow and began to roll down his face. Bingley cracked and he started running. The ground was soft and seemed to suck at his feet. A fraction of a second later there was a growl from the cougar and then he could hear its feet padding along behind him. Reckoning his time had come he plunged forward as fast as his legs would carry him, expecting at any second for the cougar to land on his back, when he heard a loud yell:

'Ahiya'a!' Ahiya'a!'

His feet struck some snag and he went head first to the ground. A second later and he could feel the cat's hot rancid breath on his neck but the expected *coup de grâce* was not forthcoming. Instead there was the sound of footsteps and then a voice.

'Good girl, Cherokee.'

There was a pause. Bingley rolled over and looked up.

'Bingley!'

Bingley's features drew into a wan smile. 'Calhoun,' he mumbled. 'Thank goodness it's you.'

By the time he had finished break-fast, which Calhoun cooked for him, Bingley was feeling a new man. Over a tin cup of steaming thick black coffee he explained what had happened. Calhoun laughed.

'That's an old one,' he said. 'Works every time.'

'I've got a lot to learn,' Bingley said. 'I guess the boys at the Crutch Bar take me for a complete fool.'

'I wouldn't worry about it. You're a greener. We were all like that once.'

Bingley was sunk in thought. 'Can I come with you?' he said. 'I could take one of your spare horses.'

Calhoun had said something about why he happened to be there with the cougar. He had set off early partly to avoid farewell scenes, leaving a note for Mary. He had brought a spare mount and a pack-horse to carry supplies; he did not know how long he might be gone.

'Appreciate the offer,' he said. 'But things could get rough. I don't think it would be a good idea.'

'Remember, I got a personal stake in this as well,' Bingley said. 'Those varmints killed my fellow travellers on the stage. They tried to kill me.'

'What about your uncle? Whatever he thinks about this snipe huntin' business he might not take it too well if you just took off.'

Bingley shrugged. 'I'm not responsible to my uncle,' he said. They sat on in silence for a while.

'I'll say this for you,' Calhoun remarked. 'You're a game one.'

'Does that mean you'll have me along?'

Calhoun looked from Bingley to the cougar which was lying a little way from the fire.

'I'm not worried about the cat,' Bingley said. He got up and began to walk towards Cherokee. It looked round at his approach and baring its teeth, growled menacingly. Bingley stopped and, thinking better of it, sat down again beside Calhoun.

'Give her time,' Calhoun said. 'Who knows, maybe you'll survive both Cherokee and the outlaws.'

Bingley smiled.

'Thanks,' said Bingley. 'You won't regret it.'

'At some point someone from the Crutch Bar will probably stop by,' Calhoun said. 'They'll see where the fire was. Leave a note for your uncle. I'll saddle the roan.'

* * *

They had been riding for most of the day and were high up in the hills. Behind them the long valley lay stretched and golden in the late-afternoon sunlight. They were both silent and Calhoun was studying the land for any sign of movement. He had noticed faded sign of riders and he knew there were a lot of gunmen gathered in the hills but so far he had not seen anyone. From somewhere ahead there was a booming sound and as they emerged from a stand of trees it grew louder. Bingley noticed it for the first time and turned with a puzzled expression on his face to Calhoun.

'Water,' Calhoun said. 'Coyote Falls.'

'Like the town?'

'Guess the name had to come from somewhere.'

They were in trees again and through occasional breaks they could see a wide sweep of country. High above an eagle swooped. Just ahead of Calhoun's dun the cougar padded steadily forward, occasionally turning its head. The trail led downwards. It was quite dark and they splashed through a shallow stream before a sharp turn took them round a rocky outcrop.

All the while the sound of the waterfall was growing louder and as they came round another bend in the trail they caught their first sight of it, pouring down over a horseshoe curve of rimrock high over their heads and tumbling in a wide curtain to a dark pool far below. Rainbows played about its upper reaches and mist wreathed in the air. The trail they were following climbed up towards it and then seemed to lead behind the waterfall. The horses were skittish and Calhoun drew them to a halt. 'See any other way?' he asked.

They both scanned the scene but there seemed to be no alternative.

'Wait here with the packhorse,' Calhoun said. 'I'll take Cherokee and scout on ahead.'

He moved forward. The noise of the waterfall was deafening and the air was drenched with spray. Calhoun was worried that the trail would be too slippery for his horse to gain a proper foothold or that it might be too waterlogged to be able to proceed. He was under the near edge of the falls and it was very dark beneath it. The dun's ears were pricked and it kept edging sideways away from the water. Calhoun moved deeper inside the curve of the waterfall, allowing his eyes to get accustomed to the darkness.

In fact conditions were better than he

had feared. The rock wall behind the falls was deeply indented and there was a considerable overhang. As he moved slowly forward he saw a glimmer of daylight and soon he emerged from behind the water on its far side. Looking back he could see Bingley with the pack-horse on the opposite side of the falls and he began to wave to encourage him to move forward.

Bingley did not seem to see him at first and Calhoun tried shouting, but the noise of the cascade was too loud. He took off his hat and began waving it and eventually Bingley saw him. He started towards the waterfall. Calhoun was still concerned about the greenhorn; he seemed to be behind the waterfall for a long time and he was just about to go back when he was relieved to see him emerge, walking and leading the horses by their reins.

'You OK!' he yelled as Bingley came alongside. Bingley nodded. 'I wouldn't like to see what that trail might be like in wet weather,' Calhoun said.

They carried on, the roar of the cataract diminishing in their rear. A wind was coming down from the higher peaks and it was beginning to grow cold. Eventually they made camp, gathering branches from the trees to build a fire. Calhoun shoved some pine cones into the flames to make the fire flare up. Then he got some bacon from the packhorse and slapped it into the pan. There was coffee and beans and by the time they had settled to eat they were feeling pretty comfortable. They could hear the sounds of running water from streams further below and, some distance behind them, the continuous booming echo of the Coyote Falls.

4

High in the Beaver Range the man known as Johnny Carver had made the deserted ruins of Elk Creek his headquarters, setting himself up in the ghost town's only hotel. Most of the rest of his gang of outlaws had taken up residence in other buildings but it was a strange place and some of them preferred to sleep in the open. The creek itself ran through a high meadow behind the town and back of it reared the snow-capped crags and bluffs of the Beavers, pockmarked with the entrances to mines long ago abandoned.

Johnny was sitting at a table in the bare saloon with two of his choice companions, Lorne Royston and Quince Lamarr; they had all ridden with Quantrill and Bloody Bill Anderson during the war.

'I just don't get this,' Carver was

saying. 'You're tellin' me that a lot o' the boys are gettin' jumpy 'cos they seen a ghost?'

'That's about the size of it,' Royston replied.

'And these are the same boys who fought their way through a war, a war we're all determined to carry right on fightin'?'

'This is different, boss. They ain't afraid of flesh an' blood. Just look at what happened down in Coyote Falls. They plumb enjoyed themselves there.'

'Coyote Falls was just lettin' off steam.'

'Yeah, but that ain't the point.'

'Point is,' Lamarr intervened, 'I'm beginnin' to feel that way myself.'

'You claimin' to have seen this ghost?'

'Nope. But I've heard things.'

'Of course you've heard things. This whole place has been deserted for years. You heard a door creak or a rat on the stairs.'

Lamarr shrugged. 'Borg says he put his rifle down while he was doin' somethin'. When he came to pick it up agin it was gone.'

'Don't you reckon it feels a mite cold in here?'

'We're thousands o' feet up in the mountains,' Carver said. 'What do you expect?'

'It don't seem like normal cold. Sometimes I go into a building and the temperature just seems to drop.'

Carver got to his feet and walked over to the bar where a few bottles were lined up. Reflected in the cracked mirror he could see the worn faces of his fellows over their empty glasses. He poured himself a drink, then returned to the table with the bottle.

'So what are you sayin?'

'I say we move out. I just don't like this place. Gives me the heebie-jeebies.'

Carver was thoughtful. He didn't give much credence to what he was hearing, but he had enough experience of leading men to know the importance of morale.

'OK,' he said. 'If it's gonna make people any happier, we'll head over the range and wait things out in an old way station I know. It ain't so handy as this for the mines, but once Watts arrives with the map we can come back again.'

'You're puttin' a lot of faith in this *hombre* Watts,' Lamarr said.

'Don't worry. He'll come through. In the meantime the boys are gatherin' together and we're hittin' pay dirt. A couple more stage hold-ups should help fill in the time. Once everyone's together and we know where to look for that buried loot we'll be ready to ride big time.'

'Those damned Yankees don't know what's comin' to them!' Royston barked. 'Man, pay-back time is surely here.'

'You got it right there,' Lamarr said.

Talk of their plans for the future seemed to settle them down. A few drinks helped to make things look a lot rosier.

'Call the boys together and I'll have a word with them, tell them we ride tomorrow,' Carver said. They finished drinking and got to their feet.

'Hope there ain't no spooks at this way station,' Lamarr said. He stopped when he saw Carver's cold gaze upon him. Next day Carver and the rest of the gang moved out of Elk Creek.

★　★　★

Calhoun and Bingley had ridden up through the hills and they were now approaching the higher peaks of the Beaver range. They travelled slowly, both because of the steepness of the terrain and because it was unknown to Calhoun. It was certainly spectacular. Ahead of them was a wide panorama of rugged mountains with snow-capped peaks disappearing into low clouds. Off to their left the land fell away to a valley hundreds of feet beneath, clothed with stands of pine, spruce and aspen.

'I never thought it would be like this,' Bingley said.

They sat their horses to admire the view.

'What was it you said made you

come out West?' Calhoun asked.

'Figured I'd set up as a lawyer.'

'Yeah? Where'd you learn about the law?'

'Boston.'

'Well, you're a long ways from Boston now.'

'Boston, Coyote Falls. It's the same law.'

'Guess so. Different set of folks though. It's applyin' it is likely to cause the problem.'

Bingley seemed thoughtful. 'Quite a contrast, isn't it?' he said. Calhoun gave him a questioning look. 'I mean between the beauty of this scene and the ways of men.'

'Never really give it much thought. Always seemed sensible to take people as I find them.'

'You fought in the war?'

'Sure did.'

'You must have seen some terrible things?'

'War changes people. There was bad on both sides. There was no accountin'' for some of it.' Calhoun looked away across the valley. 'But there weren't just bad things,' he said. 'It brought out the good in people too.'

There was a pause before Bingley spoke again. 'What do you intend to do about this man Carver?'

'It's not the first time I've been asked that question. Still not sure of the answer.'

They carried on, the cougar still loping along ahead of them.

'This is his kind of country,' Calhoun remarked.

They were crossing a high plateau when they caught their first sight of the ghost town.

'I heard some talk of this place,' Calhoun said. 'Never sure just what to make of it.'

'Is this where you expect to find Carver?'

Calhoun nodded. 'Seems strange, though, we ain't seen or heard of anyone.'

He climbed out of the leather and

reached into the saddle-bags of the packhorse to draw out a pair of field glasses which he put to his eyes. For a long while he scanned the tumbledown buildings before replacing the glasses.

'The whole place seems deserted.' He looked about and walked some little distance either side of the trail.

'There are old tracks,' he said.

'Wouldn't the cougar know if there were people about?'

'You're gettin' the hang of ol' Cherokee.' Calhoun grinned. 'Yeah, you're right. She's shown no sign of catchin' human scent.'

He took another good look about. 'We'll carry on,' he concluded. 'But keep your eyes open.'

As a precaution he took his Winchester out of its scabbard and laid it across his knee as they rode on. The only sound was the wind and the steady drum of their horses' hoofs. Just outside of town a sign lay in the dust: the words ELK CREEK were barely discernible. The town lay in a sprawl along what

87

had once been the main street. Most of the buildings were in a bad state, their roofs had fallen in and there were great gaping holes where there had once been windows. Some had collapsed completely, but most struggled to retain an upright stance, like old people bent over with age and infirmity. A few sagged and leaned together. Some were like skeletons revealing the twisted wooden bones of their structure.

'It's kinda creepy,' Bingley said.

'Just so long as there's no outlaws hidin' behind them walls,' Calhoun responded.

In fact, as he rode he could see plenty of sign that they had been here. There were tracks in the dirt of the street and horse droppings. His keen eyes saw cigarette butts and at several points the imprint of boots. They came up to the hotel, dismounted and tied their horses to the hitch rail. One of the batwings was missing and the other hung at a crazy angle. They stepped through. There were a few tables and battered chairs with missing legs. In one corner a piano gathered dust. A chandelier still swung from the ceiling and another lay shattered on the floor. At the side of the bar there were stairs, broken in places, leading to an upper floor.

Carrying his rifle, Calhoun stepped over various items of debris and began to climb the stairs. Bingley had drawn his gun and followed close behind. They came to a corridor at the top of the stairs with a worn carpet full of holes. There were rooms on either side and stepping into the nearest one, Calhoun advanced to a broken door with shattered windows leading on to a balcony.

'Be careful,' Bingley called. 'It's probably unsafe.'

Calhoun stood outside where he had a view of the street. Beyond it he could see the stream and, overlooking all, the darkening mountains. Bingley joined him.

'Nobody here,' Bingley said. 'Looks like you got it wrong.'

'The outlaws were here recently. And there's somebody still here.'

Bingley looked at him in surprise. 'How can you know that?' he said.

'Look at Cherokee,' Calhoun replied. The cougar was down in the street below, pacing about and sniffing the air. 'Besides, I seen footprints.'

'Footprints?'

'Human footprints. And they were bare.'

'I don't like this,' Bingley said.

'Neither do I. But welcome to your quarters for the night.'

They brought in the stuff they would need from their packs and tended to the horses, leaving them for the night in the rickety livery stables. The horses seemed to catch something of the eerie atmosphere and it took a deal of coaxing to settle them down.

When they had picked out a couple of the rooms in the dilapidated hotel they made supper. They could tell that both rooms had been recently used but the knowledge only served to make the atmosphere even more unsettling, at least to Bingley. Calhoun was used to long lonely nights on distant trails and he soon slept.

Bingley, however, could not relax. The dark shadows seemed filled with menace and there were disturbing and suggestive sounds, as if someone was treading on the stair or walking slowly down the empty street. There were creaks and groans as the wind rattled the empty buildings. Bingley lay watching and listening for a long time till his nervousness drew him from his bed and he walked on to the balcony. The desolate street lay below him, bathed in moonlight. The sky was awash with stars above the backdrop of the mountains.

He found himself wondering what had happened to the people who once lived here when suddenly he stiffened. Was it an effect of moonlight or had he seen for only the briefest moment a shadowy figure framed in the gaping window of a building on the opposite side of the street? He stared long and hard but could see nothing. He was almost satisfied that he had been mistaken when there came a blood-curdling howl that sent shivers down his spine. He turned and flinched as he saw a figure outlined against the sky standing beside him on the balcony.

'It's only Cherokee,' a voice said.

'Is that you, Calhoun?'

'Who else would it be?'

'You gave me a fright.'

He didn't like to mention that he thought he had seen something. He was feeling a little foolish anyway.

'Still an' all,' Calhoun continued, 'something seems to have unsettled her.'

They returned to their rooms and somehow Bingley managed to doze off. It was daylight when he came round to the smell of cooking wafting up the stairs. When he came down Calhoun had breakfast ready and it was only when Bingley had put away a good helping of bacon and beans with a couple of cups of strong black coffee to wash it down that Calhoun spoke.

'Somethin's goin' on,' he said. 'I bin down to the livery stables. Someone's been feedin' the hosses.'

'We fed 'em ourselves,' Bingley responded.

'Yeah, but not with bread an' sugar. There's traces on the floor.'

'Maybe we just didn't see it.'

'That's possible, but it wouldn't account for the fact that some of our things are missin' from the saddle-bags.'

'What things?'

'Not so sure about you, but I'm missin' a spare comb, some matches an' a shirt.'

Bingley was about to mention his previous night's experience but thought better of it.

'What do you think?' he said. 'Outlaws?'

Calhoun shook his head. 'It ain't outlaws. I found footprints. It was someone with bare feet, and female I reckon.'

Bingley's nerves had not fully recovered after his night of belated and broken sleep.

'You don't believe — '

'Nope, I don't believe in ghosts. This was no spook an' I mean to get to the bottom of it. After I've fed Cherokee we'll do a search of the buildings.'

Calhoun went off to attend to the cougar, which he had left in a room behind the counter of what had once been the general store. There were still some rusted tins of food behind the counter, some torn sacks and dusty packets of foodstuffs. As he came through the door he knew where the bread and sugar had come from but he wasn't prepared for the sight which met his eyes when he entered the back room.

Lying at full length was the cougar but she was not alone. Kneeling beside her and stroking her head was what Calhoun took to be an old woman. She was dressed in a ragged and faded calico dress. Her feet were bare; her long, bedraggled hair was brown and streaked with grey and tied behind her head with a strand of leather. At Calhoun's entry she looked up with eyes which were surprisingly bright.

'She's a nice cat. Is she yours?'

Calhoun was taken aback and it took a few moments for him to gather his thoughts. While he did so the woman continued to stroke the cougar, which seemed to be thoroughly enjoying the attention.

'Had me a bobcat for a while,' the woman continued. 'Well, not really, not like this one. He came and went but he was kind of companionable. What's her name?'

'She's called Cherokee,' Calhoun replied.

'That's a good name.'

Suddenly she stopped caressing the cougar and looked at Calhoun with alarm written on her features.

'Say, you ain't one of them outlaw varmints?' she said.

'No ma'am, I ain't. You can put your mind to rest on that score.'

Her features relaxed and a smile spread across her mouth, revealing her brown-stained teeth.

'Nope,' she said. 'I figured not.'

Calhoun wasn't sure how to proceed. 'Name's Calhoun,' he said, reaching out a hand. 'Pat Calhoun. There's a friend o' mine back in the saloon finishing his breakfast. Why don't you join us for somethin' to eat and a cup o' coffee?'

The woman considered his offer for a moment. 'That's mighty kind,' she said. 'Ain't had coffee in a long whiles. I'm Norah, Norah Carney. Seems kinda strange to say it out loud.'

She got to her feet and as she moved into the light Calhoun could see that she was not old after all — maybe in her thirties — but she looked dirty and like she'd got used to living rough.

'See you later, old girl,' she said to the cougar.

'You're not afraid of her?' Calhoun said.

The woman cackled. 'Glory be, why should I be afraid? We're two of a kind, me an' her.' She looked Calhoun up and down. 'And I ain't scared o' you neither.'

Since coming out West Bingley was getting used to surprises, but when Calhoun came in with the woman he was completely taken aback.

'Let me introduce you,' Calhoun said. 'Norah Carney, Hiram Bingley.' Bingley awkwardly put out his hand.

'Nice to meet you, ma'am,' he mumbled.

'Lords a' mercy, I ain't been called that in a long time,' she replied. She scrutinized him as she had Calhoun. 'I got a feelin' you an' me's two of a kind as well,' she said.

Calhoun scraped some bacon and grits from the pan and poured her a cup of coffee, to which she proceeded to do full justice.

'I still got me some supplies left over,' she said. 'I do a bit o' fishin' an' trappin' but it's a long time since I enjoyed chowder like this.'

'Have some more,' Calhoun said.

When she had polished off another plate of food and was on her third cup of coffee, she sat back and regarded the both of them.

'S'pose you're wond'rin what I'm doing about,' she said.

'It had got me sort of curious.'

She opened her mouth and let loose one of her hoarse cackles.

'At least you ain't scared o' me like the last lot,' she said. 'Plumb had those varmints runnin' like rabbits. Figure they thought I was a ghost.'

Bingley remembered the face at the window the previous night. 'Can't say I exactly blame them,' he said.

It was Calhoun's turn to laugh. 'I got to hand it to you,' he said. 'Last time those gunslingers tried anything, it took a whole town to beat them off. You done it single-handed.'

'Never took to 'em,' she replied. 'I knowed they was no good from the moment they started arrivin' here.' She eyed up Calhoun. 'Now if you ain't one of 'em, what business you got in these parts?'

'Unfinished business with those owl-hoots,' Calhoun said. 'We're on the same side.'

She cackled again. 'Apart from when those critters started puttin' in an appearance, I don't think I seen nobody up here for years.'

'Go on,' Calhoun encouraged her. 'What's your story?'

'Oh, it's simple enough. I used to live here with my ma and pa. They ran the general store. Then they up and died, the silver ran out and the miners drifted away. A few o' the townsfolk hung on but they left eventually. Soon there was only me. I'd got kinda used to the place. Didn't fancy heavin' up sticks. So I just sorta stuck around. I'll admit it can get a mite lonesome at times, but I can't say as I was ever one for the bright lights.'

'Tell me more about the outlaws,' Calhoun said.

'They started comin' in dribs an' drabs but it soon got to be a regular stream.'

'How many of 'em?'

'There must have been more than a couple o' dozen. One day a lot of 'em rode out; not quite so many came back again.'

'That must have been when they hit the town,' Bingley commented. 'Any idea where they are now?'

'Sure.' She laughed again. 'Still cain't get over how they high-tailed it because of one woman. Anyways, I heard them talkin'. They've moved on to an old way station down the other side of the mountains.'

'Do you know of it?'

'Sorry, can't help you there. Never bin over that way. But I can tell you what they're waitin' for.'

Calhoun made no effort to hide his eagerness.

'I heard them talkin'. They're waitin' for a *hombre* name o' Watts. He's supposed to be bringin' some sort of map. When they get their hands on it they reckon they'll be in a position to let all hell break loose.'

Bingley looked at Calhoun. 'A map,' he said. 'What do you reckon that's all about?'

Calhoun was deep in thought.

'Reckon I can answer that one too,'

the woman said. 'For as long as I kin remember there's bin rumours of a whole hoard o' treasure hidden away down one o' those mine shafts. Never give it much credence myself but that's what they're after.'

'So this map's a plan of the various mine workings?' Calhoun said.

'That's what I figure. There's bin folks before snooping about those workin's, but it's a regular prairie-dog town up there. The whole cliff face is just a maze o' tunnels.'

Calhoun looked closely at Norah. He thought he could detect a mocking tone in her voice but she only returned his gaze with a crooked smile.

'I'm beginnin' to see the picture,' Calhoun said. 'With that sort of money behind him and a whole army of disaffected ex-Rebs to back him up, Carver could wreak havoc. And not just ex-Rebs. Every horse thief, hold-up man and rustlin' backshooter would see his chance.'

'It could get a mite rowdy up here,'

the woman said. 'Ain't gonna be the same.'

'You scared 'em off once. Anyway, they ain't likely to stay round here once they get that loot.'

She looked at Calhoun. 'While you folks are settin' figurin' what to do, I think I might take me a stroll. Any objection if I take the cat?'

Calhoun laughed. 'Sure, I reckon she'd plumb appreciate an outing. I ain't got no lead though!'

'Don't need one. We'll be just fine.'

Standing at the door a few minutes later they watched the woman and the cougar as they walked away down the street, heading towards the meadows and the stream. Calhoun turned to Bingley.

'That's a remarkable lady,' he said.

'Cherokee seems to have taken to her.'

'I got me a feelin' there's somethin' she's not lettin' on about that treasure.' They watched a few moments longer till she disappeared around the corner of a building.

'I tell you what,' Calhoun added. 'With her alongside of us, I don't give much for Carver's chances.'

★ ★ ★

Later that day they walked up as far as the stream. At various points there were broken-down structures indicating where shafts had been sunk into the ground.

'Headframes,' Norah said. 'To support the hoists.'

Calhoun and Bingley leaned over the mouth of one of the shafts and peered into its depths.

'Some go hundreds of feet,' Norah said. 'Straight down.'

'It's a mite dangerous,' Bingley replied.

'Sure is. Especially if there ain't nothin' to indicate where a shaft is. I knows the place well enough but even I need to be careful.'

Beside the river they came upon another structure, consisting of a flattened circular area with a rod running out to a large heavy wheel.

'Horse-driven,' Norah said. 'For crushin' the rock.'

While they moved about the area Calhoun kept his eye out for any of the outlaws, but they appeared to have deserted the vicinity. Would Watts know about the way station? Presumably so or Carver would at least have left somebody behind.

A plan was forming in Calhoun's brain. If Carver was expecting Watts, why disappoint him? He would take the part of Watts. By impersonating him, he would have immediate access to Carver. There were weak spots. Carver might recognize Calhoun from the old days, although Calhoun realized that he had changed. Crucially, he had no map.

Then he had another idea. The map could still be a difficulty, but Bingley was a trained lawyer. He could come up with some sort of document drafted in legalese that would be enough to fool Carver. Carver had no knowledge of Bingley and it was pretty obvious that Bingley was no owlhoot. They could even ride in together.

The weak link was that Watts might turn up at any time.

When he broached the subject that evening Bingley's response was enthusiastic.

'Like I said before, those varmints owe me. I can get to work and make out some documentation tonight. By the time I've finished, those papers would fool any judge in the land.'

'Once Carver is convinced, I'll have my chance,' Calhoun said.

Bingley looked at him. Carver wasn't saying his chance to do what.

'And where do I fit in?' Norah said.

Calhoun hesitated. He hadn't thought about the woman but it only took him a few seconds to work something out.

'You take care of Cherokee,' he said. 'We can't take her along this time.'

The woman looked pleased. She laughed one of her cackles.

'Me an' Cherokee. Now that's an idea. We'll have us a real good time.'

'Somethin' else you can do,' Calhoun said. 'Keep a watch for the real Watts.'

'And what do I do if the varmint shows up?'

Calhoun and Bingley exchanged glances.

'You done a pretty good job on the rest of 'em,' Calhoun said. 'Just carry on bein' the town ghost. And if that don't scare him, I reckon the cougar will.'

5

It was easy enough to find the way station, following the trail left by the outlaws. It led along the stream and then through a pass in the mountains. Beyond that the way was steep for a while till it levelled out, then continued in a long, steady descent. Calhoun and Bingley came down through the treeline and then saw the roofs of the buildings below.

'Funny kinda place for a relay station,' Calhoun muttered.

'Maybe it had somethin' to do with the silver mines,' Bingley replied.

'Guess that must be it. Probably took a loop after leavin' Coyote Falls.'

Calhoun wasn't sure how they would be received. Normally he would have taken care to pick his way down. Now it seemed sensible just to ride straight in. Still he was wary and his hand was not far from the Winchester in its scabbard.

As they got nearer they could see that the way station was in a serious state of disrepair. It was obvious that no stage-coach had passed that way for a long time. There were also plenty of indications of its occupation by the outlaws. People were passing in and out and at one point a couple of riders galloped out of a yard and went off down the hill. Smoke was rising in a slender spiral from the chimney of what appeared to be the main building. There were horses in the corrals.

'You got the story straight?' Calhoun asked.

Bingley grinned. 'Sure have. And got the documents right here in my pocket.' He tapped his jacket.

'Don't forget,' Calhoun said.

He was thinking of another weak spot in the setup. What if Carver or any of the others were familiar with Watts? Their cover would be blown at once. But what the hell, he thought. After all, he was riding straight into the outlaws' den with a greener and a crazy woman for his sidekicks and a cougar for backup. It fitted.

He caught a glint of light among the rocks on the slope above.

'There's someone up there,' he said.

A few seconds later a shot rang out.

'Don't do anythin' stupid,' Calhoun hissed. 'It's just the welcomin' committee.'

A voice hailed them. 'Hold it right there! Put your arms up!'

'Just do as he says,' Calhoun drawled.

They put their hands in the air at the same time as two men carrying rifles stood up from where they had been concealed behind rocks.

'Throw your guns down! And be careful how you take that rifle out!'

They did as they were instructed. From behind an outcrop a couple more men on horseback appeared. One of them leaped down to gather up the discarded weapons.

'Let's take a ride,' he said. 'And remember, we got you covered all the way.'

They came down into the way station

yard where Calhoun and Bingley were ordered to dismount. As they did so the door of the main building swung open and a tall figure appeared on the veranda. He was wearing a threadbare grey Confederate jacket and a peaked cap. Calhoun gave him a quick look. There was something familiar about him.

'Carver,' one of the outlaws said. 'We found these two ridin' down the mountain trail.'

So it was Carver! Calhoun would have found it difficult to say with certainty that it was so. He only hoped that he had changed sufficiently for Carver not to recognize him. They were ushered up the steps of the veranda and into the building. There was a wooden table and a few chairs but little else. The windows were broken and there was a layer of dust on the floor. One other person was sitting on the ruins of a bunk against the far wall. Two of the outlaws followed them in.

'Take a seat, gentlemen,' Carver said. Carver had his back to Calhoun as he pulled out a chair from behind the table. He turned and sat down. Calhoun looked at him more closely. It was strange to see the man again, to see how the familiar features had been transmogrified into something else. The long hair had gone and the moustaches. He had been slim as a knife. Now he had fattened out and there was a slight stoop to the shoulders. But there was something else that was different and only when Carver was seated and looked up did Calhoun realized what it was. Carver was blind in one eye. The right eye was white and blank.

'Well,' Carver said. 'Before I start jumpin' to any conclusions, perhaps you'd better explain just who you are and what you're doin' round here.'

There was no room now for manoeuvre. It was in at the deep end.

'Perhaps I'd better make some introductions,' Calhoun began. 'My name is Watts and this gentleman is a colleague of mine, name of Bingley. He's a lawyer.'

Carver remained silent. His one good

eye seemed to bore into Calhoun.

'We have some business with a gentleman named Carver. Am I to take it that's you?'

Silence filled the room. Calhoun was nervous. He didn't like to think of how Bingley might be feeling.

'If we have come to the right place, perhaps you could conduct us to this man Carver.'

'I'm Carver.'

Calhoun glanced around at the other three outlaws. 'In that case you will be aware of what I have come about. Perhaps we could discuss matters in private?'

Carver's eye switched its gaze from Calhoun to Bingley. His mouth puckered for a moment, then he turned his attention back to Calhoun.

'You have the information?' he said.

'Mr Bingley has all the necessary documents. I think you'll find they're all in order.'

Carver looked thoughtful, then unexpectedly he leaped to his feet. His features were angry and a scar down his cheek suddenly flamed red.

'What the hell do you take me for?' he yelled. He pulled a gun from its holster. 'I ought to kill you two right where you stand.'

'I don't understand,' Calhoun began. 'Is there a problem?'

'Is there a problem? Damn right there's a problem.' He turned to the outlaw who was sitting on the bunk. 'Let me do the introductions,' he said. 'Whoever you two are, I'd like you to meet Mr Watts.'

Calhoun tried not to react, not even looking at Watts. Instead he turned to Bingley who raised his eyebrows the merest fraction.

'There must be some mistake,' Calhoun said.

Carver turned to the two outlaws standing behind Calhoun. 'Take 'em and put 'em in the shed,' he shouted. He turned back to Calhoun. 'You're gonna pay for this,' he snarled. 'I don't know what your game is but I aim to find out.'

Calhoun felt a gun in his back.

'You heard,' the man said. 'Start walkin'.'

Calhoun and Bingley were marched out of the room and down the steps of the veranda. Crossing the yard, they passed another building and continued till they came to a small outhouse, where they were thrust unceremoniously inside. The door slammed and they heard the rattle of keys.

'Well,' Calhoun said. 'I guess that didn't go so well.'

They looked about but there was nothing they could see. The place was small and very dark. There was no window and it smelled of dank hay and manure. There was a flicker of light as Calhoun scraped a match; the place was illumined for a few seconds before the match burnt out. It revealed nothing of interest. Bingley moved to the door and started to push against it.

'Here, let me have a try,' Calhoun said.

He ran at the door and kicked at it

but it was solid. After a few more tries they gave up and sank on their haunches against the wall, barely able to see one another.

'Hate to say this,' Bingley said, 'but I suffer from claustrophobia.'

Calhoun brought out his packet of Bull Durham and proceeded to roll a smoke. He offered the pack to Bingley. 'Might help take your mind off things,' he said.

Building a cigarette, Bingley took a deep draught and broke out coughing. At the same moment there came a rattle at the door and they both sprang to their feet. The door opened an inch or two and a figure slipped through it, closing the door behind him. In that brief moment of daylight Bingley thought he recognized Watts.

'Don't ask questions,' Watts said. 'They might come by at any minute.'

Calhoun was suspicious they were being set up.

'Here, take this,' Watts added, slipping a package into Calhoun's hand.

'What is it?'

'It's the plans of the mine.'

'What's going on?' Calhoun snapped.

'I'll keep this brief. That money belongs to the Government. I'm a government agent. For the moment I'm in with the outlaws, which makes it difficult to get the information out. That's your job now.'

'Why should I believe you?' Calhoun said.

'What choice have you got?' He passed something else across to Calhoun. It was a gun. 'Take this as a token I'm tellin' the truth,' he said.

Bingley started to say something but the man stopped him.

'There's no time,' he said. 'You'll just have to take my word for it. It's quiet now. I'll leave the door open. Give me a few minutes and then slip out.'

Without waiting for any further discussion, he moved to the door and in an instant was gone. Calhoun gave the door a gentle push. It was open.

'What do you think?' Bingley said. 'It

could be a trap.'

'What would be the point?' Calhoun responded. 'They got us cold as it is. We'll just have to take him at his word.'

Checking that the gun was loaded, he tucked it into his trouser belt.

'OK,' he said. 'He's had his few minutes. Let's go.'

He strode to the door and opened it a fraction. His range of vision was limited but he could see no one. Quickly he stepped through followed by Bingley. The sun had sunk behind the high mountain peaks; it was getting dark and there was a chill in the air. Keeping low and looking about them they made their way to a building behind the corrals, which looked like a stable. They were in luck. A few horses were in their stalls and hanging up at the back was some riding gear.

'Stand guard while I saddle a couple of horses.'

Calhoun quickly selected two mounts but before he could do anything further Bingley whispered to him:

'Somebody coming.'

Calhoun moved to the doorway. There were a number of outlaws heading towards the barn.

'Leave it,' Calhoun breathed. 'We'll slip out the back.'

Quickly and silently they made their way to the runway at the rear and came out at an angle of the corral. A few of the horses in the corral were jumpy and snorted but the two men had soon passed beyond the corral and into some trees at the back. Moving as quickly as they could through the undergrowth they came out eventually on to the lower slopes of a hillside that overlooked the way station.

'We'll climb and get round to the other side. At least then we'll be out of sight.'

★ ★ ★

Night had fallen. Fortunately the sky was clouded and there was little chance that anyone would spot them on the hillside. At first the climb was easy but after a time the slope angled up more steeply and it became difficult. The grass was slippery from rain or melted snow and it was not easy to maintain their footing. At one point Bingley slipped and went sliding part of the way down the hill. Calhoun looked up. The top of the hill had looked quite close from the bottom but now it seemed a long way off. A couple of times they approached what they thought was the top, only to find that it was a false summit and the hillside climbed up to further heights.

Calhoun began to edge sideways and Bingley followed his example and so they moved on and upwards by a crabwise motion. Beneath them lights were springing up at various points. Calhoun wondered how long it would take before their absence was noted. They were moving very slowly, doubled over, sometimes on their hands and knees, clutching at little patches of grass or outcrops of stone. It was very tiring and they were both struggling for breath.

Again Calhoun looked up. 'Nearly there,' he breathed to Bingley, who was a little way below him.

He waited for Bingley to reach him, then they began to climb the last few yards. It was very steep at this point and Calhoun's heart was pounding. He was searching for the best places to put his feet and all the while he could hear Bingley gasping and then muttering something beneath his breath. The top of the hill overhung a little but Calhoun's leg was over the edge and, with a final pull, he was up. Leaning over he grasped Bingley's outstretched arm and pulled him over the rim of the hillside.

They lay there on their backs till they had recovered their breath and were feeling in control again. Calhoun looked down at the way station. A light appeared, moving across the yard. It was a lantern and the person carrying it was making his way towards the corral. It moved into a darker area and then disappeared. Seconds later it reappeared and they could both hear a voice shouting something. A few more lights appeared, and then what sounded like a gong. They could distinguish shadowy forms of men moving about. There were more shouts, then a couple of men in the yard mounted horses which were tied at the hitch rack.

'They've discovered we're gone,' Calhoun said. 'Time we got movin'.'

They began to jog at a steady pace away from the direction of the way station. It was very dark, and difficult to see more than a few yards ahead. They seemed to be on some sort of level plateau with the dark shapes of hills outlined against the louring sky. Further off were the mountain ranges and, bearing in mind that they had come down from some of the higher peaks, Calhoun set his course in the opposite direction, vaguely thinking to lead any pursuit away from the silver mines and the deserted town. After a time they heard the sound of horses' hoofs still some distance away.

'They must have followed some trail which took them along the side of the hill,' Calhoun said. 'We could be making straight for them. I think the best thing would be to wait till daylight. I want to get some idea of the lie of the land.'

Calhoun could hear the sound of water and, following it, they arrived at a little hollow where some aspen trees grew.

'This will do,' Calhoun said.

There was a little spring and, squatting on their haunches, they drank from it. It was not much more than a trickle but it was cold and fresh and they felt better for it. Afterwards they hunkered down out of the wind.

'Wish we could build a fire,' Calhoun said, 'but it would be too dangerous.'

'What I'd give for a cup of coffee,' Bingley replied.

'What I'd give for a hoss,' Calhoun said.

They lapsed into silence. It was damp and cold. The leaves whispered in the wind as the two men drifted into an uneasy slumber.

★ ★ ★

Dawn was beginning to streak the sky when Calhoun awoke. He was stiff and cold and if he hadn't already been aware of it he knew now that they had little chance of survival without horses and supplies. He considered returning to the way station but it was too risky. For the present it was important to start moving to restore their circulation and stave off the cold, so, after he had awakened Bingley with a good shake, they began to move again.

The country was generally flat, grass-covered with scattered clumps of trees and stands of willow and cottonwood, indicating the presence of water. Calhoun's plan was to head away from the mountains in what he judged was the course they had been following when they came to the way station. By tending towards an easterly direction he hoped to come round the side of the hills and then work back towards the town of Coyote Falls.

He didn't want to involve Norah in further trouble by heading that way and he felt reasonably comfortable about her and the cougar. If they made it back to Coyote Falls they could return to the disused diggings with a posse. He wondered whether the marshal had recovered from his injuries and what Mary was doing. It wasn't the first time she had been on his mind.

Towards mid-morning they heard the sound of horses once again. Calhoun indicated some boulders and they hid behind them. From their position they had a good view over the country which sloped gently downhill and presently they saw riders coming towards them up the incline. Calhoun drew the gun from his belt. He noticed for the first time that it was an old-fashioned Whitneyville Walker, .44-calibre, large and heavy. It seemed an odd choice but he had no time to think about it.

'Now's our chance to get us some hosses,' he whispered.

As the riders came closer he could see that there were three of them. He checked the cylinder. Three riders, six shots. Not much room for error.

'There's nothin' you can do,' he said to Bingley. 'Just stay down out of sight.'

He looked back at the approaching horsemen. Something was wrong. They had drawn to a halt and one of them was pointing in their direction. Another one produced a rifle. The next moment there was a flash of flame followed by a booming reverberation among the rocks and Bingley's hat went flying into the air.

'You idiot!' Calhoun breathed. 'I told you to stay out of sight.' As an afterthought he added: 'Are you OK?'

'That hat cost me sixteen dollars,' Bingley replied.

Another shot rang out and went whistling just over their heads. Calhoun waited. Next moment a whole fusillade of shots went singing into the rocks and Calhoun ducked as a ricochet kicked up shards of granite near his head. Still Calhoun did not reply. He needed to make every shot count. He was hoping that the riders would carry on coming, perhaps believing that he was unarmed, but they had slipped from their horses and were taking shelter behind some trees and bushes in a little dip in the ground. It was a good position and it was hard for him either to be able to see them or get a decent shot in. One of them might be able to outflank him by crawling to his right under cover of the slight ridge which continued in that direction.

'Keep a lookout to the left!' Calhoun shouted to Bingley.

Shots began to ring out and Calhoun was tempted to reply, but he realized he would probably be wasting his bullets. Then he had a thought. If the gunmen were in a position to outflank them, maybe they could do the same. The horses were standing a short distance away from where the gunmen were concealed. If they kept real low they might be able to slither their way towards them. The ridge would work to their advantage. Quickly he explained the plan to Bingley.

'They don't know for sure whether we are carrying arms,' Calhoun said. 'They're a little confused. That gives us an edge.'

He was talking up the situation for the benefit of the greener, but, to give him his due, Bingley didn't show any trace of fear or reluctance.

'This time really keep low and follow me,' Calhoun said.

On his belly, he slithered out from behind the rock and began to work his slow way towards the horses. There had been a few moments of respite from firing but now shots began to ring out, whining among the rocks they had just vacated. Just as well, Calhoun reflected. There was a big danger of ricochets back there. Very gradually they continued to work their way forward.

The grass was just long enough to provide cover although Calhoun had known Indians who could stay concealed where there was no grass at all. He had learned something from them. He knew how to find directions even from that angle of vision and he had no doubts that the two of them would fetch up where he wanted.

The outlaws were still firing in the direction of the rocks so they had not detected anything so far. They were still protected too by that slight ridge which, while it offered concealment for the outlaws, also served to disguise their passage. Calhoun could hear Bingley's heavy breathing from behind. He was starting to find things difficult. Calhoun stopped for a few moments to give him a rest, reminding him again to stay as low as possible.

'Now I know what a snake feels like,' Bingley said.

'Just hope we don't run into a real one,' Calhoun whispered.

They slid forward once again. Now

Calhoun could smell the horses, then, through the grass, he could see their legs. One of them began to blow and Calhoun, raising his eyes, could see that they were getting restless as they sensed the presence of two men in the grass. Now was the moment of real danger. They would have to leap to their feet and dash the few remaining yards to the horses, running the gauntlet of the outlaws' fire. They would need to spring aboard as quickly as possible and ride as hard as they could away from the barrage of shots that would follow them. Calhoun explained all this to Bingley.

'Are you sure you know what to do?'

Bingley nodded.

'OK. Now!'

In an instant they were both on their feet and running pell-mell through the grass towards the horses, but they hadn't gone more than a couple of steps before the outlaws realized what was happening and turned their fire on them. Shots pinged through the air and tore up the ground around them.

The horses were on the move, jostling one another in their fear and edging sideways. One of them went down, neighing as a stray bullet caught it. Calhoun was abreast of a big palomino and with one bound he was in the saddle. Bingley's foot was in the stirrup of a bay but it was beginning to buck and he was having a problem getting on board.

For a moment Calhoun thought he was going to fall, but the next moment he had succeeded in swinging his leg over and they were off, turning their horses away from the trees and bushes where the outlaws were concealed.

A barrage of shots banged out in their rear and bullets went whining close by. Calhoun instinctively twisted in the saddle to return fire, but then he remembered how little ammunition he had available. Slapping the sides of the horse with his hat and applying his spurs, he rode on just behind Bingley whom he had allowed to take the lead.

Bingley was a good rider, however, and soon they were beyond range of the pursuing fire.

Allowing their horses to slow to a trot they carried on riding till they struck an east-west trail and drew rein. There were tracks in the trail dust indicating that riders had passed along it fairly recently, and Calhoun was reminded that they were still deep in enemy territory.

It was a pity that the riders had taken their rifles from the scabbards. It meant that Calhoun still only had the Whitneyville Walker for weaponry. However there were strips of jerky in one of the saddle-bags and, on reaching a brook, they decided to stop and eat. They took the horses to the water and filled up the canteens. By the time they had finished they were feeling a lot happier.

They set off again. They were still going downhill, although the slope was gentle. Presently they came to a point where the trail they were following branched and a thinner trail led down to a more substantial stretch of water than they had come across so far. They rode their horses into the water. Calhoun knew that anyone with any expertise in following sign would be able to pick up their trail quite easily but he doubted that any of the outlaws would be so skilled. The further along the stream they rode, the higher grew the slopes on either side.

'I reckon if we follow this down we'll come out on level ground at the foot of the hills. If we circle south and west it should bring us round the shoulder of the hills back towards town,' Calhoun observed.

'Reckon it'll take us mighty close to the Crutch Bar,' Bingley replied. 'I wonder if my uncle got that message?'

Calhoun thought for a moment. 'Yeah, you could be right,' he said. 'Sounds easy but there's still a whole parcel of gunslicks between us and the ranch and they'll be doing their damndest to get their hands back on that map.'

He paused. 'Goldarn it,' he said. 'I'd

clean forgotten about that map. I reckon it's about time we took a look at the thing.'

They carried on riding. Night was descending and it was getting dark in the coulee. Eventually they halted, stripped the saddles from the horses and made camp beside some flat rocks.

'OK,' Calhoun said. 'I think it's about time we took a look at the map.'

The light was fading fast but there was still enough for them to see. Calhoun reached into his pocket and brought out the little wrapped parcel. He carefully undid it. Inside was a folded sheet of paper. Calhoun opened it out, expecting to find the plans to the mine and the treasure it contained. Instead there was a scrawled message written in pencil:

The Falls. Saturday 29th September. Noon.

Calhoun looked at Bingley. 'What the hell?' he said.

'Check that there's nothing else,' Bingley replied.

Calhoun looked carefully inside the pouch but it was empty. 'No plans, no map,' he said. 'What do you make of it?'

Bingley took the piece of paper and read the brief message once more. 'Looks like it's been written in a hurry,' he said, 'and torn from a notebook.'

'What's today's date?' Calhoun asked.

Bingley thought for a moment. 'The twenty first, I think,' he answered. 'I ain't too sure.'

'Eight days,' Calhoun said. 'I don't know what this is all about, but I guess we'd better be at Coyote Falls by then.'

Early next morning they rode on, following the course of the stream which was bringing them out into a widening valley. Away to their right a spur of the hills jutted out into the flatlands and their way would lead round it. Calhoun was watchful, studying the trail ahead and the slopes on either side. Bingley was more thoughtful, considering the strange message on the paper. They had talked about it for a good while the previous night but it still made no sense to either of them. Suddenly Calhoun pointed ahead.

'Riders,' he said. 'Plenty of 'em.'

Bingley looked where Calhoun was indicating.

'To the right, comin' along the spur.'

Bingley saw them. They were riding almost parallel to them but high up along a ledge. Presently they disappeared from sight.

'They'll have seen us,' Calhoun said, 'and they'll be lookin' to cut us off at the spur. We got two choices. Either we turn back or we try and beat 'em to it.'

'The Crutch Bar lies in this direction.'

'Yeah. Let's dust.'

They splashed the horses across the stream and set off at a steady trot. Calhoun didn't want to exhaust their mounts, but to keep something back in reserve for when they would really need it. The spur of the hills lay not more than three miles away. It would be a question of who reached it first.

A shot rang out from high above but the outlaws were too far off for it to present a problem. Probably one of them had caught a glimpse of them and tried a chance shot. Presently the outlaws emerged into view again. They drew to a halt and then some of them began to urge their horses down the hillside. Apparently they had decided to get down at this point but the slope was too steep and they gave up the attempt. Regaining the ground they had lost, they bunched up with the rest of the gang.

They were riding in a fairly tight formation except when they strung out to avoid an obstacle. Sometimes they disappeared from view only to emerge once again further along. Occasionally there was a flash of sunlight from their rifles. They were ahead of Calhoun and Bingley but they would have to ride down the spur of the mountain.

Calhoun looked anxiously at the trail ahead, concerned that another group of riders might appear, cutting off their route. They were getting close to the spur now. Shots were being aimed in their direction and some of them were dangerously near. The outlaws had reached the highest point of the ridge and were about to start their descent.

Calhoun decided that the time had come to put their horses to the test. Calling to Bingley to follow him, he applied his spurs to the palomino's flanks and set off at a dead run for the angle of the spur.

The outlaws, perceiving what was happening, spurred their horses forward, but it was more difficult for them as they had the slope to contend with. Calhoun and Bingley had chosen two good horses. They were galloping ahead at a fast rate and the spur was coming up at a startling speed. Foam was flying from their horses' mouths as they ran flat out with no sign of any breaks in their rapid stride.

The wind whipped at their faces. Shots were raining down off the hillside. A bullet zipped by Calhoun's head. He glanced sideways. It was going to be touch and go who won the race.

Reaching down, he drew the Walker from his belt and for the first time in two encounters with the outlaws he returned fire. A horse went down, throwing its rider who went bouncing head over heels down the hillside till his headlong passage was halted by a large boulder. Still it looked as though the outlaws would outrun them. Then Calhoun realized that the angle at which they were approaching was deceptive and that the outlaws had further to go than he had thought. There were ridges in the long slope of the hill which couldn't be seen from below.

With a whoop Calhoun and Bingley were round the end of the spur and galloping across the range lands beyond. The first few of the outlaws were reaching the flats behind them. A bullet whistled past and then another embedded itself in the leather of Bingley's saddle. His horse veered to one side but then, startled, picked up even more speed and went thundering on.

Calhoun turned and fired. His bullet found its mark and the leading horse shied, then slowed almost to a halt. The horse behind clattered into it while a couple of others veered round. In the moments of confusion that followed Calhoun and Bingley made further ground on their pursuers. Calhoun's concern was for the horses. They were still charging on and showing no sign of slackening, but for how long could they keep it up?

But then the outlaws would have to ask themselves the same question. Some of the pursuers were fanning out but Calhoun was not concerned. Instead, he regarded this as a sign that the outlaws were getting desperate, attempting to outflank them. He pondered whether to take another shot but the outlaws had fallen behind and it wasn't likely he would be successful firing at that range from a plunging horse.

Bent low over their horses' manes they rode on, the horses' hoofs drumming a muffled rhythm, their flanks lathered and their breaths starting to come in great heaves. Calhoun took another look behind but there was no sign of their pursuers. After galloping a little further, he gave the signal to stop and allow the horses to blow.

'What do you think?' Bingley gasped. 'Reckon we've outrun them?'

'Yup, for the time bein'.'

Calhoun looked around. There was a stand of cottonwoods a little way ahead but not much else. In contrast to the country they had been riding through this was flat and featureless.

'We'll haze 'em over to the trees,' Calhoun said, knowing there would be water there.

They let the horses rest and drink, and then rode out again, keeping the hills on their right, riding into the declining sun and letting the horses go at their own pace. They had been riding like this for what seemed a long time when suddenly Calhoun stiffened. Ahead of them was what looked like a cloud smudged against the skyline.

'Another bunch of the varmints,' Calhoun said.

'What do we do now?'

'Our only chance is the hills.'

They turned their horses and urged them to a trot. The hills now looked a long way distant and there was no knowing whether their pursuers might not have gone that way. But the land the other way was wide open and offered no sort of refuge.

Despite their rest the horses were tired and it soon became apparent to both men that this time they were not going to get away. The dust cloud had resolved itself into a group of riders and they were coming on at quite a pace. Calhoun hefted the Walker. He had only four bullets left. It was a hopeless case but at least he would take some of them with him. Thinking this, he was suddenly surprised by a hoarse laugh from his companion.

'What's so funny?' Calhoun said.

Bingley laughed again and Calhoun thought that maybe he had flipped with all the strain they had gone through.

'Keep ridin',' he urged.

Bingley's laugh subsided into a cough before at last he could speak.

'No need for that gun,' he said. 'Those ain't outlaws. Those are Crutch Bar riders.'

Calhoun looked hard at the band of men who were fast approaching. Sure, there looked to be something about them. One of them waved his hat. They drew to a halt and Bingley broke into a laugh again.

'That's Orne Thompson,' he said. 'And the big man ridin' right alongside him is Ray Cole. They're a couple of my uncle's top men.'

They drew to a halt and soon the riders came alongside.

'Howdy,' Bingley said.

'Howdy,' Thompson replied. 'Hell, you sure took the long way back to the Crutch Bar.'

'Guess they were mighty ornery snipe,' Bingley replied.

The ranch hands looked at one another and then burst into laughter.

'Let me introduce you to my friend Pat Calhoun,' Bingley said.

'Sure am glad to make your acquaintance,' Calhoun added.

6

High up in the mountains Norah Carney had just returned from exercising the cougar.

'Sure is getting a mite cold,' she said. 'You an' me, we don't feel it too much but I reckon time's come to build us a good fire.'

Out back of the general store she kept a pile of wood torn mainly from the ruined buildings of Elk Creek. She gathered an armful and returned to the back room of the store, where she laid it in the grate. She lit one of the matches that she had stolen from Calhoun and set it to the wood. The match burned down and she tried another.

'Jumpin' Jehosophat!' she exclaimed. 'I know what we need.'

She went to a cupboard, pulled out a metal box, put it down on the floor beside the cougar and opened the lid.

Inside there were bundles of dollar bills and papers. She took a handful and placed them around the pile of wood.

'That should do it!' she said, applying another match.

It worked. Before long she had a good blaze going. She sat down beside the cougar and began to stroke the side of its head.

'This is nice,' she said. 'You an' me, we do just fine. I wonder how those other two are gettin' along? Guess they'll be back by an' by.'

The cougar growled and rolled over on its side while Norah moved to a rocking chair beside the hearth where the treasure burned.

Calhoun had returned to town, leaving Bingley at his uncle's ranch. Neither of them had come to any conclusions about what the message might mean, but it certainly pointed to something happening on the given date.

As he rode away from the Crutch Bar Calhoun felt a strange sense of excitement and anticipation and by the time he approached the town it had developed into an unwonted nervousness. He almost felt inclined to give the Graysons a miss and book himself a room at a local boarding-house, but he realized that he was being foolish.

As he rode down the main drag he took notice of the work that had already been done in his absence to repair the damage wrought by the fire. The place was looking a lot better. The worst of the ruins had been cleared away and people were busy carrying out repairs. Where the fire-blasted saloon had stood was now a gaping empty space.

He tied his horse outside the marshal's office, knocked on the door and stepped inside.

'Calhoun! You're back!'

Calhoun hadn't been sure whether he would find the marshal there. He had underestimated Grayson's powers of recuperation. The marshal was already behind his desk and he managed to get to his feet at Calhoun's approach.

'Goldurn it! It's good to see you,' he said.

'Good to be back,' Calhoun said. 'You're lookin' in pretty fine shape.'

'Right as rain,' the marshal replied. He pointed to the crutches propped up against a wall.

'Still need 'em now and then,' he said, 'but I'm just about back on my feet. Turns out the injuries weren't as bad as the doc liked to make out.'

Calhoun laughed. 'Maybe so,' he said.

Grayson brought out the bottle of bourbon and two glasses he kept in a drawer and poured out a couple of generous drinks.

'You'd better tell me what happened.'

Calhoun sat down opposite the marshal and took a long swig of the whiskey. He had just started to tell his story when the marshal interrupted him.

'I can't tell you how pleased Mary will be to see you. She's been worryin' so much.' He paused. 'You know, she thinks a lot of you. She's my sister. I know her about as well as anybody I guess.'

His words made Calhoun realize how much he had been missing Mary. 'I think a lot of her,' he replied.

The marshal shot a quizzical glance at him. 'Better get on with the story,' he said.

Calhoun explained as quickly as he could what had happened. When he had finished the marshal pursed his lips and whistled.

'Phew!' he said. 'You sure don't go about things the easy way.'

He poured them both another drink. 'One way and another,' he said, 'that outlaw nest is gonna have to be cleaned out.'

Calhoun nodded.

'What about ol' Cherokee?' the marshal said. 'You must be gettin' worried.'

'She's in good hands,' Calhoun replied. 'Still, I bin missin' her.'

There was silence for a while, then the marshal resumed:

148

'What do you make of this map business? I mean the message. Sure seems strange to me.'

'Likewise,' Calhoun said. 'Neither Bingley nor I could make any sense of it.'

They considered the matter for a while. Then the marshal scratched his head.

'Reckon this is one for Mary,' he said. 'But whatever happens, you can count me in for the twenty-ninth. Come on, I ain't doin' much good around here. Let's get back to the house.'

Calhoun felt a return of the strange nervousness that he had felt on the trail from the Crutch Bar. He untied his horse and walked it down the street alongside the marshal, who reluctantly took up his crutches. For some reason Calhoun was worried about what Mary's reaction would be on seeing him, as if the events of the last few days might have served to divide them.

He need not have worried. She must have seen them coming along the street because she ran out to meet them even before they had reached the gate in the wicket fence, and when he held her in his arms it just seemed the natural thing to do.

'Pat,' she said, addressing him by his first name. 'We've missed you. Come inside. I've got coffee brewing on the stove.'

A few minutes later Calhoun felt real good to be sitting on a comfortable settee with a cup of black coffee in his hand.

He glanced round the room. Mary's handiwork was everywhere in evidence from the cushions and antimacassars on the chairs to the flowers in their vases and the looped curtains at the window. It was homely and comfortable and Calhoun envied the marshal his domestic comforts. As they sat together he repeated what he had told the marshal.

'What do you make of it?' Grayson asked his sister. 'Sure is a funny state of affairs.'

Mary held the paper with the message in her hand and read it through for the third time.

'What do we know of the facts?' she said. 'The man who gave you this claimed to be a government agent. I don't see any reason at present to doubt that.'

'That's pretty well what I said to Bingley,' Calhoun said.

'Presumably he infiltrated the gang in order to get the information about the whereabouts of the treasure. He couldn't get away, but why would he scribble this message and what could have happened to the map?'

'And what's the significance of Coyote Falls?' the marshal interjected.

'The question seems to be whether the note is a general statement or whether it was aimed specifically at Mr Calhoun,' Mary continued.

Calhoun looked up at her.

'If it was aimed at you,' Mary said, addressing him directly, 'then it must have been written by somebody who recognized you, somebody who knew you.'

Calhoun considered her words carefully. 'Yes, you're right!' he exclaimed.

'Take another look at the writing. There's not much to go on, but could you recognize it?' She passed the paper back to Calhoun, who looked at it intently before shaking his head.

'It's no use,' he said. 'Besides, I don't reckon I'd be able to recognize anyone's writing even if there was a lot more of it.'

'Think back. Did you recognize the man who helped you escape?'

'I can't remember anything about him,' Calhoun said. 'It was dark in the shed and things happened quickly.'

'You said you saw him earlier.'

Calhoun sent his mind back over the episode at the way station, when he had been surprised by the introduction of Watts. A memory flickered.

'There was something,' he said.

'Think hard. It could be crucial.'

Calhoun's face was a picture of concentration. He was trying to bring the whole scene back to life: the room, the people in it, especially Watts. Watts — or the government agent — had been sitting on a bunk at the back of the room while he talked to Carver. He tried to picture what the man had looked like but it was hopeless.

Then he suddenly found himself thinking not about Watts but about Carver. At the time he had been struck by how much Carver had changed — how he had put on weight, lost his hair and his moustaches, become blind in one eye. He could almost have been a different man.

Then he recalled how the scar down Carver's face had blazed up in anger when he realized that Calhoun was trying to deceive him. He had seen a scar just like that before, but not on Carver's face. That scar had belonged to Con Reeder!

Suddenly Calhoun's whole perspective shifted. In a moment of revelation he suddenly saw what must be the truth. The expression on his face was such that even the marshal noticed it.

'What is it?' he asked.

'You've thought of something?' Mary

said. 'Something important.'

Calhoun began to speak, shaping his thoughts even as he put them into words.

'Yes, I've thought of something. I remember now. The scar down Carver's cheek. When Carver got annoyed the scar showed up. But it wasn't Carver. It was Reeder who'd had that scar. Why didn't I think of this before? I thought Carver had changed, but I still assumed it was him. But in fact it was Reeder. That scar was the only real identifiable feature.'

The others were regarding him with uncomprehending looks on their faces. Calhoun was getting excited.

'Don't you see? I thought Carver had betrayed Reeder. But it must really have been the other way round. Reeder was credited with setting up the escape route. In fact he was leading people into enemy hands all the time. And not just refugees like me but Unionist sympathizers of various sorts. It was a good way of flushing them out.

'Carver must have realized what was going on. He wasn't there at the end of that last trip across the mountains because Reeder must have had him removed. Reeder wasn't killed. He wanted it to look that way. Instead he took over Carver's identity. It could make things a lot easier for him in the aftermath of the war.

'No doubt he had made enemies. To be identified as a Union supporter could also open doors and give him cover for this whole mad exploit of carrying on the war.'

'So what do you think about the map?'

'The map was simply a ruse to get the government agent, whoever he is, into the outlaws' nest with direct access to Reeder. If it exists it's probably worthless.'

'But Mary thought that message was aimed at you,' Grayson remarked.

'And you've already said you didn't recognize the man.'

'That doesn't matter. Whoever it is he

wants me to be at Coyote Falls at that time and on that day.'

'Well, whatever this is all about, you won't be alone this time,' Grayson said.

Mary gave him a frowning look. 'You won't get far on those crutches,' she said.

'I got time,' he replied. 'I'll be there.'

'I'll have Bingley along,' Calhoun said. He laughed. He had been going to make a joke at Bingley's expense, but then he stopped himself. Bingley had come through it all pretty well. He might be a greener but he had grit.

Mary shook her head. 'I think you're all crazy,' she said. 'But I'm pretty well used to it now.'

She stood up and, leaning over, poured out second cups of coffee for her brother and Calhoun.

'Tastes good,' Calhoun said.

He felt comfortable. There had been no need to feel apprehensive about returning to Coyote Falls. He felt at home and he had no doubts now that there was something between him and

Mary. No need to rush things. Let them take their course.

It was only later that he found himself thinking about the Walker that he had been given, and which he had now swapped for his own Colt Army .44s. Despite being outdated and unwieldy, it had once been Carver's choice of weapon.

The next day Calhoun set off early to ride up to Elk Creek. It felt good to ride alone and he was thinking that when the time came for the rendezvous at Coyote Falls he might prefer it that way. Although he was alert to the possibility of ambush he saw nothing of the outlaws. Presumably they had returned to the way station on the other side of the mountain. The waterfalls seemed fuller than the last time and he guessed that there had been rain or snow higher up.

It was when he had reached a point between the falls and the deserted town that he suddenly felt wary. His horse was restless and its ears were pricked.

Something was upsetting him. Calhoun took the Winchester from its scabbard. As he came to a halt he looked about him. Everything was still except for the breeze and the creak of his saddle as he swung down. Ahead was a little patch of brush filled with flickering shadows and patches of sunlight. Calhoun had the feeling that something was moving in there.

He led the horse to the side of the trail, he hunched down beside a thicket and raised his rifle. Listening intently, he thought he could hear a rustling sound, then abruptly the bushes parted. Calhoun's hand closed on the trigger of the Winchester but just as he was about to fire he dropped the weapon and rose to his feet.

'Cherokee!' he shouted.

It was the reddish-brown form of the cougar that had emerged into the sunlight. The cougar sprang forward and jumped up at Calhoun, almost knocking him to the ground.

'Steady, old girl!' He laughed.

The cougar leaped up at him again, then turned and began to walk back towards the bushes. She turned and, drawing back her lips, snarled and then let out a roar.

'What is it?' Calhoun said.

The cougar was acting strangely and Calhoun looked towards the bushes, bringing his rifle up to his waist. The cougar moved on before stopping further up the trail. Calhoun lowered the rifle, satisfied that there was no one lurking in the bushes. He stepped to the palomino, placed the Winchester back in its scabbard and swung into the leather. The cougar was quite a way ahead and Calhoun knew that something was amiss. Normally the cougar would walk just ahead of him. The only thing to do was to follow the animal.

'Seems like she's tryin' to tell me something,' he muttered to himself.

Calhoun got his first clue to what was wrong when they reached the ghost town and there was no sign of Norah. Calhoun had expected her to come out and meet them. Sitting astride his horse in the middle of the empty street he called her name, but there was no reply. He would have begun a search through the deserted buildings but the cougar seemed to want to move on. He dismounted and glanced in at the general store and the saloon, but there was no sign of her other than the burnt-out fire in the grate. The cougar was growling and running in circles. Calhoun got back on his horse and trailed the cougar as it turned and ran down the street.

'Looks as though she's headed for the workings,' Calhoun said.

Following the cougar he rode up past the stream and the remains of the diggings towards the pot-holed cliff face beyond. Snow had fallen and the place was dusted with white. Heavy clouds lay atop the mountain peaks and it seemed there was a lot more snow on the way.

The cougar was slinking along the line of the cliff. It was quite rocky; Calhoun dismounted and leaving the horse in a sheltered patch, followed the cougar on foot, taking his Winchester with him. The cougar was making strange noises and running in a distracted kind of way before stopping at the entrance to a tunnel leading into the cliff face. It let out another roar as Calhoun approached.

'Easy, old friend,' Calhoun said.

As he came up to the tunnel entrance he bent down to examine the ground. Although they had been dusted over with snow he thought he could detect traces of the imprint of boots leading away from the tunnel in the opposite direction. He peered inside. The roof was low; it was dark even by contrast with the gloomy atmosphere outside and he could not see very far.

The cougar had entered the tunnel ahead of him and cautiously he began to follow her. The walls were damp, the floor was uneven and in places there were falls of rock. At intervals wooden struts supported the walls and roof. The atmosphere was musty; when Calhoun touched one of the walls there were patches of damp.

The tunnel took a slight bend and then it was almost completely dark. His eyes had adjusted and he could just make out the shape of the cougar ambling down the passage ahead of him. The cougar stopped and began to growl. In the enclosed space the sound was magnified. Coming alongside Cherokee, Calhoun could see that there was a kind of alcove built into the rock.

'In here?' Calhoun said.

He struck a match. In the brief illumination he could see a dim shape slumped against the far wall. Quickly he strode over, lit another match and bent down.

'Norah!' he said.

She was lying on her side and her hands and feet were tied. For a moment he thought she was dead. Just then, however, she startled him by turning her head and looking at him. Her hair was matted with blood and a line of congealed blood ran down from her brow almost to her chin.

'Calhoun!' she said. 'You took your

time gettin' here.' The cougar had advanced to her side and began to lick her with a rasping tongue. 'Good girl, Cherokee,' she said. 'I knew I could count on you.' She turned to Calhoun. 'Is she OK?'

Calhoun had scarcely gathered his scattered wits.

'Cherokee?' he replied. 'Sure. But what happened? Are you badly hurt?'

'There's a candle somewhere,' she said inconsequentially.

Calhoun looked around. The candle was lying almost beneath her. He picked it up and lighted it.

'Bin comin' in these mines for I don't know how long an' never had no trouble,' Norah began. 'I can't remember. Somebody musta slugged me. Tied me up but I managed to shuffle this far. Anyway, what're you waitin' for? Get me out of these bindin's.'

Calhoun pulled a knife from his jacket and quickly cut her loose. She sat up and began to rub her arms and legs. Calhoun glanced around. What he had thought was an alcove was in fact a side shaft which stretched a considerable distance before turning a corner and being swallowed in darkness.

'What were you doin' in here?' Calhoun said.

'I know most o' these old workin's. Knowed the men who dug 'em. They don't hold no fears for me. Never had nothin' like this happen to me before though.'

'Let me look at your head' Calhoun said.

Taking care to be gentle, he examined the wound to the back of her skull. There was a big swelling and a nasty gash.

'Does it hurt?' he asked.

'Got me quite a headache but it'll be OK. How's my noggin?'

Calhoun smiled. 'I guess you got a thick skull,' he said. 'Come on, let me help you up. I got water in my saddle-bags.'

Norah looked at him. 'Best be careful,' she said. 'I can't say for sure just how long I bin lyin' there but whoever did this could still be around.'

'I don't think so,' Calhoun said, remembering the traces he had found outside the tunnel.

When she got to her feet Norah winced with pain and staggered when she put a foot forward. Calhoun swung the rifle across his back.

'Here,' he said, 'put your hands around my neck.' When she had done so he lifted her in his arms.

'Lordy,' she said, 'I do declare I'm beginnin' to blush.'

Calhoun laughed.

'Excuse the liberties,' Calhoun said. 'Come on, Cherokee. Lead the way.'

It didn't take them long to reach the entrance to the mine and make their way to where Calhoun had left the palomino. After sitting her on a rock he got the water and the bandages and began to clean up Norah's wound. When he had finished and her head was bound with a strip of cloth the sun was well down in the sky. He brought his flask of whiskey from his saddlebags and offered it to Norah. She tipped it back and took a long pull.

'Don't normally drink a lot of liquor,' she said, 'but that sure does hit the spot.'

'Any idea who might have done this?' Calhoun said.

Norah shrugged. 'Nope, but things just ain't been healthy round here for some time.'

'Must be quite a change for you.' Calhoun grinned. 'All this time you had the place to yourself and suddenly it's become a holiday resort.' Calhoun helped her up on to the horse's back and they set off for Elk Creek.

As they rode Calhoun was thinking hard. Norah Carney was a tough lady and made light of what had happened to her, but he wasn't fooled. Whoever had attacked her had left her tied up in the deserted mine without food or water. She would have died had it not been for the cougar and her own resourcefulness. What Calhoun wondered was whether her attacker intended coming back for her, and the more he thought about it the more likely it seemed. What reason could he have for slugging her? It didn't make sense.

And then another thought occurred to him. How had he managed to avoid the cougar? The two thoughts merged to provide an explanation. The attacker had slugged her because of the cougar. Whatever he wanted from her, it could wait. He hadn't wanted to face the beast, even with a gun in his hand. Suddenly Calhoun recalled Norah asking him if the cougar was OK. It hadn't registered at the time. Now he asked her what she had meant.

'I can't think,' she said. 'My head feels all dizzy.'

'Try to remember.'

Her face puckered up with concentration. 'I think there might have been a shot,' she said.

Calhoun drew to a halt and jumped from the saddle. He called the cougar to him and examined her more closely. Sure enough there was a burn along her side which had singed some of the fur. She had been grazed by a bullet. After stroking her and whispering some soothing words, he climbed back behind Norah. He had a pretty clear idea of what must have happened, but the question of the attacker's identity remained. There was one way to find out. Go back to the mine and wait to see if anyone showed up.

Night had fallen by the time they were settled in back at Elk Creek. Calhoun had decided to visit the mine early the next morning as there seemed little chance that Norah's attacker, whoever he was, would return before then. Norah still felt a little groggy and her head ached.

Calhoun had questions he would have liked to ask but in view of her condition he let it pass. Whoever had attacked her must have had a reason for doing so. What did he think she might know?

Calhoun built a fire and prepared something to eat. Afterwards he explained his plans to Norah. At first she was keen to go with him but in the end she was persuaded to stay. Calhoun was counting on the element of surprise. The presence of the cougar might be likely to give the game away and it would be better if he left Cherokee behind.

'You be careful,' Norah said. 'There's a maze of tunnels. A body could easily get lost.'

Calhoun nodded, running his hand over the recumbent cougar's fur. It was a puzzling situation but maybe he would know a lot more before the morrow was over.

7

Only a faint lightening of the cloud-filled skies indicated that dawn was at hand when Calhoun walked out next morning. He had decided to leave his horse behind at the ruined livery stable. It was no great distance to the mines and he wanted to be as inconspicuous as possible.

It was chilly and a few isolated snowflakes fluttered down on the bare land as he came past the heavy wheel of the rock-crusher. Up ahead the walls of the mountain loomed threateningly. He half-wished he had brought Norah along with him. He knew the entrance to the tunnel but she might have been useful to have along with her knowledge of the diggings. Then he thought better of it.

He certainly missed the cougar. She had been a good companion on many a solitary trail. He was feeling more than a little dispirited. He wasn't looking forward to re-entering the mine and he realized that he might be on a wild goose chase. There was no guarantee that whoever had attacked Norah would return to the scene. He could be in for a long, lonely vigil.

As he walked he kept a sharp lookout for sign but there was nothing. The faint traces of the tracks he had seen previously were gone. He had brought candles with him but he was not keen to light them until it was necessary. Besides, if there was anyone in the tunnel he didn't want to give himself away. With a final glance about him he entered the tunnel.

Going slowly and careful not to make any noise, he made his way down the passage to the intersection where he had found Norah. She said she had crawled some distance from where she had been felled and Calhoun started to make his way down the second tunnel.

Although it was dark, the blackness

was not profound. He wondered whether light might be getting through from outside somehow and then, turning another corner, he had his answer. The tunnel widened out into a small cave. Its walls were sheer and high above him he could see a pinpoint of light probably from some kind of exit on the mountainside.

He saw all this in an instant, but it wasn't till his eyes had accustomed themselves to the dimness that he saw the real feature of the cave. There was someone seated with his back propped against the far wall! Calhoun had taken care over his approach and whoever it was seemed not to have noticed his arrival.

Calhoun drew his gun and edged nearer, keeping close to the wall and scarcely breathing. Whoever it was did not stir. Maybe he was unconscious. Calhoun decided the time had come to act.

'OK!' he said. 'Don't move. I got you covered.'

There was no response.

'Don't try to be cute!' Calhoun rapped. 'Just stand up away from that wall and do it real slow.'

His words rang oddly in the empty chamber. He waited but there was still no response. He stepped forward again, his gun at the ready. As he got closer the man's face seemed to glow a strange white as the thin illumination caught it from overhead. Calhoun's nerves began to jangle and then he drew up with a flinch. It was not the eyes of a living person which stared back at him but the empty sockets of a grinning skull.

He drew back, then, gathering himself, paused to take a closer look. The skeleton was seated with its bony hands interlocked. It was dressed in the tattered remnants of a red shirt and threadbare trousers and it wore a broad hat on its head. Someone must have placed it there. By its side lay a rusted pick.

Calhoun's instinct was to flee the

place but he forced himself to step forward and look at the remains more closely. Who was he and how had he died?

Calhoun suddenly felt a powerful wave of repugnance for the ghost town, for the mine workings and for everything connected with this haunted mountain top. He longed to be back at Coyote Falls, to be back with normal people, with the friends he had made, with the marshal and Bingley and most of all with Mary Grayson. All he wanted was to escape, to get back down the mountain, but first he had to return to that accursed ghost town and collect the cougar and his horse.

He turned away but even as he did so he thought he heard something moving in the tunnels beyond. His nerves were raw and he suddenly realized that his hand was shaking. He was almost inclined to think it might be the ghost of the dead man come to seek what was left of his mortal existence, but then the sound of a footstep snapped him back to his senses. Whoever was out there, it wasn't a ghost or an apparition but a man.

He drew his gun and slunked back into the recesses of the cave. There was a scraping sound; something was being dragged along the stone floor of the tunnel. His attention was focused now. After all, wasn't this why he had come out to the mine? As long as he stayed calm, the mystery of who had attacked Norah Carney would soon be solved.

He expected the man to come right into the chamber but the footsteps had halted in the corridor beyond. For a time there was very little movement and then the scraping was resumed. Suddenly there came a loud hammering which made him start. The hammering soon ceased and the footsteps receded, but he could still hear occasional furtive movements which diminished until there was silence once again.

Calhoun waited, crouched down behind some rocks at the back of the cave. The minutes ticked silently by. He was undecided about what to do. What was going on out there? Still he waited, listening intently for any further sounds which might give him a clue as to what was happening.

At last, convinced that it was no use waiting any longer, he rose cautiously to his feet. In the same instant there came a huge crashing roar of sound and a shock wave that drove him back against the rock wall. A vivid flash of light illumined the darkness and then he remembered no more.

When he came round his ears were ringing and there was blood coming from his nostrils. He felt dazed and confused and there was a pain across his chest. He was lying on his back and where his head lay a trickle of blood oozed out on to the rocky floor. For a few moments he did not move, then very gingerly, fearful of what he might find, he began to raise himself up. The pain in his chest subsided and putting a hand to the back of his head he felt a swelling and a cut which accounted for the loss of blood.

Slowly he stood up and examined himself. As far as he could tell there was no serious damage. He could move all his limbs and the constriction in his chest was gone. He was breathing naturally and except for the pain in his head and the ringing in his ears he was OK. He remembered the flash of light and the thunderous noise but he still felt confused and didn't understand what had happened.

As his head cleared and his eyes adjusted to the gloom he picked his way forward. There was dust in the air and the smell of explosives. Suddenly fear began to gnaw at his vitals like a hungry rat.

Staggering through the cave he arrived at the tunnel and began to move along it. Smoke hung in the air and he knew what had happened. The man he had heard had dynamited the outer tunnel. He knew what he would find when he reached it. On arriving at the intersection he turned towards the mine entrance, hoping against hope that he might be mistaken. But it was no good. Just a little way along the path was blocked by a huge mound of rock and rubble. Calhoun stopped and stared.

It was hard to make anything out because the passage had become so dark. He rushed forward and began to claw at the mountain of rock which now lay between him and the outside world. He looked up. The roof had collapsed and what had been the tunnel was now completely choked with debris. Trying to remain calm, he began to try and pull out individual rocks, but he soon realized it was useless. There was no way past the blockage. He was trapped in the mine.

He sat down on the floor, desperately trying to remain calm. If he panicked he knew he was lost, but he found himself reliving that episode in the war when the bomb exploded and left him badly injured.

He was back in the orchard, looking up at the sky while the tears ran down his cheeks. It was all vivid again; he was back there lying on the earth like a crippled animal while the searing pain scorched through him. Then he was crawling once more inch by inch to the burnt-out farm building. But more than anything else there was that empty blue sky. It was the memory of that sky which brought him back to a consciousness of his present situation. How beautiful it had seemed.

Would he ever see such a sky again? What must he do to find it once more? Breathing deeply to control his nerves, he forced himself to consider the options.

Norah had told him that the tunnels and shafts ran for long distances. He had candles and matches to see by. If he followed the tunnel it might lead to another exit. On the other hand it was more likely that he would get lost in the depths of the mountainside. If he waited, sooner or later Norah would realize something was wrong and come to investigate. But what could she do?

There was no way through from the other side of the obstruction.

He had brought some pemmican with him and a flask of water. There was no immediate problem in that regard, but his supplies would not last for long. He sat and turned things over in his mind till at length he came to a conclusion. The only possibility of escape lay in climbing up the walls of the cave and reaching that ray of light entering from the outside world at the summit of the funnel. But it was a forlorn hope. He had been struck with the steepness of the walls. They had looked sheer. But he had only gained a general impression. He had not looked at them in detail. Maybe there would be some way up. He pulled a candle from his jacket pocket and lit it. The flame burned up and its flickering aureole of light only served to emphasize the emptiness and darkness of his surroundings. Holding it up, he made his way back down the inner tunnel to the cavern where the skeleton had lain. The shock of the blast had blown it away and what was left of it lay in separate bits, partly covered by the dust and debris of the explosion. The ray of light seemed a long way off and the cavern walls looked almost perpendicular in places. Calhoun's heart sank. It seemed impossible even to attempt the climb.

Circling the cavern, he started to examine the walls more closely. The candle shed only a limited light but it was enough for him to see that in places they were not as sheer as he had at first thought. There were sections that offered the possibility of being able to get at least part of the way up. It was impossible to see higher. He would just have to take his chances when he reached that stage.

After circling the cavern he chose a spot which seemed to offer the best possibility. The rock wall was sheer but a little way up there was a narrow chimney. Finding a small fissure he squeezed his fingers into it and hauled himself upwards. Raising his right knee he wedged his foot against the rock while his other foot found a tiny foot-hold. He looked up to find another fissure and repeated the process, approaching the chimney at a slight angle. If he could wedge himself into it he might be able to work his way up.

He reached up and swung his leg outwards, searching for a hold. There was a ledge barely wide enough to put his toes on but he had to chance it. At this point there wasn't far to fall. Securing his foot as best he could, he moved further up till he was right next to the chimney. It was narrower than he had thought when looking up at it from the floor of the cavern but he was just able to squeeze into it, his feet jammed against the wall on either side. He was half turned and needed to get his back against the rock wall. It was a difficult move but he accomplished it.

He was now facing outwards, his back against the rock. Slowly he began to work his way upwards keeping his legs and feet jammed against the sides of the chimney. Despite the cold he was soon sweating from the hard physical task of inching his way upward. Already the cavern floor seemed a long way below. He could barely see it in the darkness. His shoulders ached from contact with the hard rock but slowly he moved up the chimney.

As he did so it began gradually to get wider and he found it more and more difficult not only to move but to maintain his position. His legs were straddled and his hold was becoming more and more precarious. Twisting his head, he glanced above him. The chimney opened out and on one side there was a ledge. If he could work his way up to it and then push himself on to the ledge he might be able to reach higher. Gritting his teeth he forced himself upwards till his head was clear of the chimney and his shoulders were against the ledge.

The next part would be painful. Still pushing with his feet, he arched backwards. His shoulders scraped against the rock but his coat offered some protection. He reached up in an attempt to find some extra purchase. One of his legs was hanging free and with the other he made a last desperate push against the chimney wall. His contorted upper body was perched precariously on the ledge as he shuffled to try and move along it.

For a moment he thought he was going to fall but then his waist was over the ledge at the same time as his hand found a sharp protuberance to cling on to. He clutched tightly at it, not registering that the palm of his hand was flowing with blood where the pointed rock bit into it. Another shuffle and he was safe for the moment, lying on his back on the ledge nearly halfway up the cavern wall. Carefully he managed to jack himself into a sitting position from which to calculate what his next move should be.

He got to his feet and, holding close to the rock wall, he inched his way along the ledge. Above him the wall receded but the angle was less steep. There was also a little more light. Having ascertained as far as he could how best to proceed he began to reach for the next level, searching for holds for his hands and feet. He could no longer see the floor of the cave which was swathed in blackness. It was just as well or he might have suffered from vertigo. As it was he felt like a fly clinging to the wall, straining his eyes to see where the next move should be.

Slowly he inched upwards, making reasonable progress, till suddenly he was presented with a real problem. Above him was an overhang. He looked for an alternative route but his vision was limited and he could not see one. There was only one option. He would have to somehow heave himself over the edge, relying on the strength of his arms.

Getting as close as he could to the lip of the overhang he reached up till his arms were over the lip. Now was the crucial moment. He would have to let go with his feet and rely on the strength of his arms and shoulders to haul him over. If the ledge above was insufficient for him to lie on he would plummet to the cavern floor.

For a few moments he stood there. His throat was dry and he swallowed hard. He thought of Mary before pressing down with his shoulders and taking his feet from their holds in the rock. The strain on his shoulders was intense and he heard them crack with the effort. Putting out all his remaining strength he hauled himself up, his feet kicking against the rock.

He was almost halfway there and his upper torso was over the lip. He leaned forwards, straining with all his might till his legs came over the edge. He reached up to try and pull himself forward, pushing his body into the surface of the rock. He began to slip and desperately sought for purchase. One foot slid back but the other wedged against something solid and gave him more to push against.

Gasping with the effort he moved upwards an inch or two. His hands grasped and held to something firm and with another desperate heave he was safe. Trembling with the exertion he lay face down while he recovered his strength and his nerve. The ledge went back for some distance and he began to slither forwards till he felt more secure. Then he lay, trembling throughout his body, trying to summon the strength for a last push towards the light which was now tantalizingly close.

When he felt sufficiently recovered he examined his position. He was not far from his goal. The problem was that just a little higher the walls of the cavern started to close in to form a kind of funnel and there seemed no way he could scale them. At the highest point, just below the source of light, he would be hanging virtually upside down.

He lit the candle and held it out. Now for the first time he saw that there was a rope dangling in midair. It came down to just below the level of his head and hung over the black chasm beneath him. What was it doing there? He could only surmise that someone had used it to climb down to the cave from the hole in the mountainside above, perhaps before the tunnel had been excavated. What had happened to the rest of the rope he had no means of knowing. Now only the frayed ends remained.

Calhoun continued to examine the rock walls but there was no way he could ascend the inverted chimney. His one chance lay in seizing hold of the rope but it was too far out for him to reach. His only option was to launch himself into space and hope to clasp the rope. It was a jump of about six feet and there was no room for a run-up. It would have to be from a standing position on the narrow ledge. More than that, he had no means of knowing how securely the rope was attached. If it had been there since before the mine itself what were the chances of it still being firmly enough fastened to bear his weight? Would it have survived the ravages of the weather high on the exposed mountain side? Still, it was his only chance and there was no point in thinking about it.

He rose to his feet and stood precariously on the high ledge. When he blew the candle out he could barely perceive the rope and his every instinct told him not to attempt the crazy leap. Once, twice, he tried to summon the courage but he failed at the crucial moment. His stomach was fluttering and his knees were shaky. Below him was a black void. It was asking too much of himself to leap into it.

Then he began to have further doubts. He still carried a slight stiffness in the left arm and shoulder from his war injuries. Would he have sufficient strength to hold on to the rope and then haul himself up it even he succeeded in grabbing it? He was still suffering from the effects of the latest blast.

He moved his feet and a dislodged stone went plummeting over the ledge to land with a strangely loud noise on the cavern floor below. The sound seemed to shake him out of his reverie. Taking a long deep breath and crouching slightly to give him impetus, he sprang from the ledge, reaching up as he did so. For a moment he seemed to hang suspended in space, then his outstretched hands found the rope and grasped it. There was a jarring shock but he held firm as he swung like a spider from its web in the vault of space.

Now that he had the rope in his grasp he was afraid to relinquish one hand's hold but the growing ache in his shoulders forced him to do so. Taking his left hand from the rope, he raised it above the right and, seizing the rope firmly again higher up, began to haul himself up. Putting all the powers of his strength and concentration into the effort, he repeated the process until he was high enough to be able to wrap his legs around the rope. He felt more secure now but the rope was swaying giddily. Slowly but steadily he continued to climb, hand over hand, grasping the rope firmly between his knees.

After a time he looked up. Light was pouring down on him like water from the hole in the cavern roof; he was ascending through a stream of blessed air. It gave him fresh energy to climb the last few yards and then drag himself through the aperture. His shoulders scraped against rock and earth and he was free.

For a few moments he lay gasping on the ground, and then he raised himself to his feet. He was standing on the side of the mountain about two thirds of the way up. Below him was the high plateau with the river running through it and away beyond the ruined buildings of Elk Creek. It was a dull day and cold with low hanging clouds presaging snow but to Calhoun it was perfect. He felt the wind on his face and, unable to contain his relief and joy at having escaped from that deadly cavern, he began to shout and holler. For the second time in his life he felt the tears run down his cheeks. This time they were not tears of pain but tears of sheer joy.

When at last he had calmed down he bent to examine the rope. It was wrapped around a rock and badly frayed. He sank to his knees, quivering with the realization of how just close he had come to hurtling to his death on the rocky floor of the cavern. He breathed a heartfelt thanks to whoever had fastened the rope into position.

Then he realized that he had solved the mystery of the skeleton. It was the same person who had fixed the rope and by so doing saved him from a miserable death. The man must have been one of the original prospectors. He had located the presence of silver and lowered himself into the cave to explore further. On his way up or down the rope had frayed and split, propelling him to certain destruction. Calhoun could only hope that he had not suffered. But what a terrible end!

He guessed that it was Norah who had discovered him and sat him up against the wall of the cave. He had a momentary feeling of revulsion. She was a strange lady. With one last look all about him he began to pick his way down the mountainside.

By the time he got back to Elk Creek the weather had broken and snow was falling heavily. He found Norah in her customary place, sitting beside an empty grate with the cougar by her side. The animal leaped forward to greet him. Norah looked up at his approach.

'Find anything?' she said.

Calhoun threw her a questioning look. 'Nope,' he replied. 'Leastways not the identity of the man who slugged you.' Norah looked as though she was about to say something in reply but, after a pause she merely added: 'You look plumb tuckered.'

'It's a long story.' She was right. He was feeling exhausted. The details could wait.

'Here,' she said. 'Sit down. Put your feet up. Reckon you could do with some chow?'

Calhoun nodded.

'Let me fix you something.' She got up and Calhoun sank into the vacant seat.

'Gettin' chilly,' she said. She went out through the door and returned with an armful of wood. 'Build up a fire,' she commented.

Calhoun was dozing. She went to the cupboard, drew out the metal box and returned with it to the grate, where she proceeded to line the wood with dollar bills. She struck a match and applied it to the flames. The cougar licked Calhoun's hand which was hanging over the side of the chair and he opened his eyes.

'Be warm right soon,' Norah said. She threw in a few more bills. Calhoun sat up to stroke the cougar. He looked into the fire and a puzzled expression slowly spread across his features.

'What are you doin'?' he said.

'Makin' a fire. I don't notice it much myself, but I reckon you'll be feelin' the cold.'

Calhoun leaned forward. 'But what's that you're lightin' it with?'

'Paper. Takes a time to get started.'

Calhoun was suddenly alert. He sprang to the fire and reaching into the gathering flames, pulled out a charred note.

'This is a hundred dollar bill!' he said.

Norah looked at him uncomprehendingly.

'A hundred dollar bill,' he repeated.

Her expression did not change and suddenly he burst into laughter.

'How long have you been usin' paper like this to light the fire?' he said.

She shrugged.

'Don't you realize?' he began, then he broke into laughter once again. 'Those paper things are Federal greenbacks.'

He was feeling a little hysterical and his laugher was infectious. Soon Norah had joined in and it was some time before they could stop.

'You mean you've been lighting fires with dollar bills all this time?' he breathed.

'Been lightin' fires whenever I needed to keep warm,' she replied.

Calhoun looked at the metal box.

'There were quite a stack of 'em,' Norah said. 'I found 'em up in the mine. Cost me a lot of effort to bring down. Probably more of 'em in there still.'

'If so, they're gonna stay there,' Calhoun said.

He sat down again and leaned his head against the back of the chair. He cared about as much for the treasure as Norah did and he wanted to relish the moment. All this commotion about the treasure was for nothing. Reeder had tracked it to these mountains and gathered his gang of gunmen with the aim of using it to finance his deluded ambitions and carry on fighting the Civil War. Even if the map existed and indicated its location, he was way too late. Norah Carney had already found it and used the money as firelighters. He looked at her with renewed admiration. She was a one-woman fighting force.

'I'll go and fix us that grub,' she said. 'Yes, and somethin' for you too, Cherokee.'

While she was out Calhoun had another revelation. He had been thinking about the explosion at the mine. He had been working on the assumption that it had been aimed at him but now he thought differently. It would have been rather an extravagant way to get rid of him. And if the treasure was within those workings, why would anyone want to destroy the means of entrance?

That was the clue. Whoever had set off the explosion had been deliberately seeking to seal it off. He had not known that Calhoun was inside. Nor, presumably, had he known about Norah Carney. And the man who seemed to have the clue as to where the treasure was concealed was Watts, the man who had set him and Hiram Bingley free and pressed that cryptic message in his hand.

Calhoun wished he had observed him more closely. He had only the vaguest impression of the figure sitting in the corner at the way station. But he was suddenly convinced that he was the man behind the dynamiting and that, if he was right, he was no government agent since the government would have no interest in destroying the access to the treasure. Leaning back he chuckled once more when he thought about Norah having beaten them all to it and her own personal use for the loot.

After a short time she returned with a steaming plate of beans and potatoes and a tin mug of black coffee.

'You don't seem to run short of supplies,' Calhoun said.

'Reckon as how those gosh-durned outlaws might be missin' some,' she replied.

'All part of your ghostly activities, I suppose,' Carson said.

He set to with a will. When he had finished Norah surprised him by asking him to accompany her to the livery stable.

'It's snowin' some,' Calhoun said. 'We just got ourselves comfortable.'

'It'll only take a minute,' she replied.

Calhoun put on his jacket. When they stepped outside a bitter wind was blowing and the snow crunched under their feet. Norah had condescended to put on a threadbare jumper but otherwise she seemed unaffected by the weather. The livery stable was only a little way down the street and when they got there Calhoun took the opportunity to take a look at his palomino and the remaining packhorse. They seemed in good shape. Evidently Norah had been doing a good job of looking after them.

After he had spoken a few words to the horses she led him out the back where there was the broken down fence of a corral. Lying propped up against a post was the body of a man. He lay in the shelter of the livery stable wall but snow had drifted over him. Calhoun had not been prepared for the sight and stepped back in alarm.

'Caught him sneakin' up on the hosses,' Norah said. 'Likely he's the one hit me over the head.'

Calhoun took a closer look. The man's face was tipped up and he recognized him as one of the men who had been present at the way station.

'Reckon you could be right,' he said. 'Seems like he was takin' an opportunity to do a bit of treasure huntin' on his ownsome.'

'Yes. I figure he returned. When he didn't find me he came on here.'

The man's throat had been torn out.

'He came at me,' Norah said. 'It was Cherokee saved me.'

'I guess he had no way of knowin' just how close he came to the treasure,' Calhoun murmured. 'That is, if you've any of it left.'

She shook her head. 'Used most o' them boxes up,' she replied. 'Helped me through quite a few winters. At times it gets kinda cold even for an old spook like me.'

8

Marshal Jim Grayson was sitting at his desk when the door burst open and three men walked in. They were Jake Adams, the owner of the Crutch Bar, and two of his men, Orne Thompson and big Ray Cole.

'Howdy,' Grayson said, looking up from some papers on his desk.

'Mornin',' Jake replied. He glanced at the crutches leaning against the wall.

'Don't need 'em any more,' Grayson said.

'Good,' Adams replied. 'Because I reckon it's damn time we did somethin' about that no-good gang of outlaws hidin' in the hills.'

'You know,' Grayson replied, 'I was just about thinkin' the same thing.'

'They've done enough damage,' Adams said. 'Look what a mess they made of this place. And I'm way past bein' annoyed at my cattle goin' missin.'

He glanced at his two ranch hands. 'Not to mention they almost killed my nephew,' he added.

'How is Hiram?' the marshal said.

'He's fine.'

'He's shapin' up good,' Orne Thompson added. 'We'll be sorry to see him leave.'

The marshal gave Adams an enquiring look.

'Only as far as town,' he said. 'Finally found some premises. Settin' himself up as a lawyer. It's what he intended doin'.'

'I guess you know what happened to Hiram and Pat Calhoun,' Ray Cole said.

'Sure.'

'They got the low-down on where those no-good skunks is hidin' out,' Adams said. 'What do you say we put a posse together and ride out there?'

'It's what I had in mind,' the marshal replied.

'I can get together a bunch of my boys,' Adams added.

'Good. I'll put word out around town

and rassle up a few more. Pat Calhoun is out of town but will be back directly. Let's say we ride day after tomorrow at sun-up?'

The matter settled to everyone's satisfaction, Marshal Grayson wandered over to his sister's café. She looked up expectantly at his arrival.

'Any sign of Mr Calhoun?' she said.

'That sounds a bit formal. Nope, but he'll be back soon enough.'

His words couldn't stop Mary from worrying. While she was out back preparing something for the marshal to eat, he looked out of the window. Things were pretty much back to normal in Coyote Falls. The burned and shattered buildings were already well on the way to repair and where the saloon had stood a new building was in process of erection. The marshal didn't know it yet, but Hiram Bingley had already earmarked it for his law offices. As he looked up the main street the marshal's eyes narrowed. Just coming into view were two riders. One was Pat

Calhoun but he couldn't make out the other. As they came closer he could see that it was a woman.

'Well I'll be goldurned,' he muttered.

He thought twice about calling to Mary, but then he remembered what Calhoun had told him about the strange lady of the ghost town and his mouth curled in a smile. That was who the other rider must be.

'Mary!' he called.

She appeared in the entrance to the kitchen.

'Calhoun's back,' he said.

He didn't get up from his table to welcome him. Mary was already out of the door and he figured it might be better to leave the field to her.

Later, when they were all back at the house that the marshal shared with his sister, and Norah had retired for the night, Grayson told Calhoun about his meeting with Jake Adams and his men earlier that day.

'You mean to ride the day after tomorrow,' Calhoun said. 'Seems to me that should tie in real well. I aim to be at Coyote Falls at noon on the twenty-ninth. They won't be expectin' anythin' to happen before then. We should catch 'em by surprise.'

'You won't be headin' up there alone,' the marshal said. 'Whatever happens, this time you'll have backup.'

When the day came the posse set out, picking up men from the Crutch Bar and following the trail round the mountain spur that Calhoun and Bingley had ridden. Bingley seemed to be very chirpy. He had been accepted by the hands at the ranch and he was about ready to set up in town. They rode on and topping a rise had their first glimpse of the way station. It was still some way off and there was smoke coming from the chimney.

'There it is,' Calhoun said.

The marshal turned to his men. 'Everybody ready? We'll ride as far as that clump of trees and leave the horses there. After that, spread out and surround the place.' He gave orders as to where each member of the group should position himself.

'I'm gonna give those owlhoots one chance to give themselves up, but I don't expect they'll take it.'

They rode into the trees and tethered the horses, then moved stealthily forward on foot. They were on the lookout for signs of movement, but so far they had not detected any. There were sounds of horses from the stables. The smoke from the chimney rose in a thin plume and disappeared on the breeze.

They slipped quietly and stealthily through the thin cover and when they had reached an appropriate point they separated to take up their allotted stations.

Grayson moved forward till he had a good view of the front of what must have been the old eating-house, then eased into position and waved the others on. He had an occasional glimpse of one of them, but they were good and kept themselves concealed. He calculated the time it would take for each of them to take his place, then added seconds and minutes. He checked his weapons and placed them ready for use.

Now that he was back in action he felt good. He took his rifle in his hand, raised himself slightly from the ground on which he was lying, and called loudly to the building.

'Listen up! We have the place surrounded. Come out with your arms raised.'

His words reverberated in the air. A few birds flew up from behind the barn. The ensuing silence seemed almost tangible. The marshal waited. There was no sound from the building.

'Come out now! Throw down your weapons.'

Again there was silence. Then an answering voice barked:

'Who are you?'

'Remember Coyote Falls? Well, it's payback time.'

'You must be crazy,' the voice yelled.

Quiet resumed. Calhoun was watching closely for indications of activity from any of the way station buildings, but there was none. He looked about. There was no sign either of the posse.

'I'll give you one more chance to give yourselves up,' Grayson shouted. 'The place is surrounded. You've got no choice.'

Again silence enveloped the scene like a blanket. A spider crawled over Grayson's arm and he flicked it aside. He was tempted to call again and deliver an ultimatum but he desisted. After all was said and done, he would prefer the matter to be decided peacefully. He wanted to give them every chance.

Then suddenly all further reflection was ended as the eating-house suddenly erupted in a crescendo of firing and bullets screamed above his head. From the direction of the barn another burst of shooting rang out.

'Right men!' he called. 'Let them have it!'

His voice was lost in the tumult of noise, but there was no need for him to give orders. From all around the perimeter of the relay station rifles cracked and bullets thudded into the walls of the eating-house and the barn. Flame stabbed through the empty windows as the inmates returned fire. Over Calhoun's head bullets sliced through the branches of trees and scattered a shower of debris all round him. His rifle was empty. He jacked more shells into the chamber and resumed firing.

From somewhere a scream rose above the clatter of gunfire. Somebody had been hit. Turning his attention to the barn, he saw a figure briefly outlined in the doorway and rapidly squeezed off a shot. The man reeled back. Smoke was rolling over the buildings and the air was pungent with the smell of gunpowder. From the direction of the stables came the sounds of horses tramping and neighing. There didn't seem to be any firing from that quarter, which indicated that none of the owlhoots was inside.

Calhoun had an idea. If he could work his way round to the stables, not only would he have a much better angle on the eating-house, but he might be able to loose the horses. The outlaws would then be stranded. He resolved to act quickly in case the outlaws had a similar idea and decided to make a rush for the stables. Blasting off another round, he began to crawl on his hands and knees through the undergrowth.

Bullets were tearing up the ground around him, but in general the outlaws were aiming too high. He didn't know how much ammunition they had available, but they were wasting a good deal of it. He reached the edge of a patch of high grass and paused to weigh up the situation. It was not far to the corner of the stables, but there was a stretch of open ground he must cross, when he would be exposed to fire. On the other hand, the stables were at an angle to the outhouse and the open space might be something of a blind spot.

There was no option but to chance it. Taking advantage of a lull in the firing, he doubled up and began to sprint towards the building. He had covered about half the distance when shots began to ring out. Bullets thudded into the ground and plumes of dust rose into the air. A bullet whistled past his ear and slammed into the stable door. Splinters rained down and one caught him just below the eye, drawing blood, but he was across now and in the shadow of the stables.

Panting for breath, he reached the doorway. The door was hanging open and, remaining in the shelter of the wall, he peered inside. It was too gloomy within for him to be able to make anything out except some of the agitated horses in their stalls. Just then a bullet shattered the far doorframe and without taking further thought Calhoun flung himself inside.

He rolled to the shelter of one of the stalls and waited while his eyes grew accustomed to the darkness. The far end of the stables was open to the day and his eyes soon adjusted. As he had surmised, there appeared to be no one in the stables.

Outside, a horse appeared in the frame of the runway. Very slowly Calhoun raised himself to his feet. Bullets were thumping into the walls. The outlaws had spotted his run and there seemed to be a sudden concentration of fire on the stables. He ran to the door and returned fire before coming back to begin freeing the horses. There were eight of them and outside he guessed there were more.

His experienced hands worked quickly, but it took time and the horses were spooked. One of them, a big chestnut, was kicking against the wall. As Calhoun approached it reared and began thrashing out at him with its sharp hoofs. He stepped back and slipped in the mire. The horse reared over him and as its forefeet came down he rolled to one side. The hoofs came down within inches of his face.

Quickly he was back on his feet as the chestnut broke loose and began to buck. He made a grab for the horse's halter rope and pulled it hard. The struggle was intense, but he succeeded in pulling till the horse's head was down and he was able to blindfold it with his bandanna. Then he held the horse by its ears, talking to it, until it had quieted to the extent that he was able to remove the blindfold and let it go. Tossing its head, it made for the runway and charged through the open end of the stables into the fields beyond.

Working feverishly, Calhoun had the horses out of the building, then he ran to the open rear of the stables. From there he had a sideways prospect of the back of the eating-house. Firing was less intense at this point. Calhoun knew that Bingley and another one of the Crutch Bar men had it covered. He wondered whether they had spotted his run for the stables.

He snapped more cartridges into his rifle, took aim at the window frame and fired. From the sloping ground beyond the fields Bingley and the Crutch Bar hand began a new hail of fire. There was a crashing sound from within the eating-house and suddenly Calhoun saw flames begin to lick around the edges of the window frame. Smoke commenced to billow from within the building. There was shouting and then a fresh burst of shooting. The flames were spreading and smoke was pouring from the roof. Suddenly a pillar of fire burst through the roof which had been thatched and then sodded with a layer of earth from which weeds and grass had grown. The conflagration was out of control now.

'Get out!' Grayson shouted. At the top of his voice he called to his men to hold their fire.

'Give yourselves up!' he called, but there was no response from the blazing building.

Suddenly there was a cacophony of gunfire and from both the front and back doors of the eating-house men came bursting, firing as they ran. They were heading for the stables; then they halted in confusion when they realized that the horses had been loosed.

'Throw down your guns!' Grayson shouted in a last desperate bid to make them give up the struggle, but the only response was a fresh burst of firing from the outlaws. Bullets went crumping into the walls of the stable and the air sang with their passage. One of the outlaws saw Calhoun in the open frame of the stables and raised his weapon to fire. Calhoun's rifle cracked an instant before the outlaw's, and he went backwards as the slug tore into his chest.

The gunslicks began running again, still firing. Then from the surrounding posse there came a responding haze of fire that sent them sprawling dead and injured in the dust of the yard. Calhoun was blazing away now when from the corner of his eye he spotted a man running towards one of the horses. Turning, he fired and the man went down, clutching his leg.

'All right!' the man shouted as he lay prone on the grass. 'No more! We give ourselves up.'

There was some sporadic shooting, then the roar of the guns ceased. The outlaws began to throw aside their weapons and put their hands in the air. Behind them the flames had almost destroyed the eating-house. The roar of the furnace was now loud in their ears and a burning wall of heat made the atmosphere dance. Calhoun emerged from the cover of the stables, his rifle at the ready.

'Quickly!' he called to the remaining outlaws. 'Get away from there. Make for the open meadow.'

The outlaws began to walk disconsolately away, dragging their wounded comrades with them. Grayson called to his men and they came out from their places of concealment, advancing cautiously. Calhoun moved carefully forward. It seemed the fight was over, when suddenly from the direction of the barn a shot rang out and then another. Calhoun felt a searing pain in his shoulder and fell to the ground.

Even as he did so he was cursing himself for having forgotten the man in the barn. He pulled himself up on one leg just as a figure emerged from the barn at a run. He was moving quickly. It was not far to the shelter of the trees and he might have made it had he not turned to fire back at the men in the yard. Calhoun raised his rifle, conscious of pain as he did so. The man was almost into the trees but before Calhoun had a chance to squeeze the trigger there came a muffled report and, throwing up his arms, he went pitching forward, impelled by his own momentum, and crashed face first to the ground.

The observers looked at each other in consternation. For a moment Calhoun thought the man had simply tripped and fallen. He expected him to get to his feet at any moment. He continued to lie prone, however, then the figure of Bingley emerged from cover. He bent over the inert figure on the ground, then he reached up and waved. There was a pistol in his hand. Calhoun lowered his rifle and clutched at his shoulder. Blood was still trickling from the wound to his face. Looking away from Bingley he saw Grayson running towards him.

'Where are you hit?' Grayson shouted.

'I think it's OK!' Calhoun called back. 'It's just a graze.'

One of the Crutch Bar men grabbed him under the arms and started to drag him backwards. Calhoun could not help wincing with pain.

'I'm sorry,' the man shouted above the crackling flames, 'but that building is about to collapse.'

Calhoun made an effort and managed to stumble away with the man's support. Even as he did so a figure appeared in the doorframe of the building, fire-blackened and grim. It came slowly forward, a gun still held in its burned and clawlike hand, walking with a slight limp. One of the outlaws gasped.

'It's Carver,' he said.

The others were looking at their

barely recognizable leader with expressions of fear and revulsion on their faces as with infinitesimally slow movements he raised the revolver. Nobody moved. They were rooted to the spot in horror. Time seemed to have slowed to a stopping point. Slowly, slowly the gun was being levelled when the building suddenly emitted a creaking, groaning sound almost as if it were a living thing and then fell in upon itself with a mighty showering of sparks and ash, burying the outlaw leader within it.

Smoke rose into the air in dense clouds. Spluttering and coughing, covered in grime and ash, the men pulled their neckerchiefs about their mouths and noses and staggered away from the burning building while Grayson supervised the rounding up of the gunslicks. Only one of the Crutch Bar riders had been injured and two of the townsmen, but none of their wounds was serious. Calhoun had lost blood and was in some pain, but after Bingley had looked at his shoulder more closely he was able to confirm that it was nothing much more than a burn.

'You've been lucky,' he said. 'Nothing's broken.'

Bingley was giving a tolerable impression of being in his element and Ray Cole was almost tempted to remind him about the snipe hunt. He refrained but tipped a wink in Calhoun's direction. The surviving outlaws were led to the empty barn prior to being taken back to the town of Coyote Falls. Grayson was figuring just where he would keep them all till the circuit judge came by.

The horses were rounded up and saddled. When Grayson was satisfied that all the outlaws had been accounted for, allowing for the fact that some of them had probably been elsewhere to begin with, the posse was ready to return to town. As they rode out the main building was still smouldering and a powerful stench of burning filled the air. The fire had spread but most of the other buildings had survived.

The men were in jubilant spirits. The

town was avenged and they had come out of the affray remarkably well. The only thing that worried Calhoun was what had become of Watts but if he was right in his assessment of what had happened at the mine, then Watts had managed to absent himself from the way station. It didn't seem likely that he would have come back.

He turned to say something to Bingley but he was riding behind with some of the Crutch Bar hands. It didn't matter. Soon Calhoun forgot about Watts and found himself thinking of Mary instead. After all, she was what really mattered now.

The appointed day arrived. Calhoun rode slowly and easily towards the hills. He was alone. Bingley and Grayson had both been keen to accompany him but Calhoun had turned them down. He had a feeling that whatever destiny had in store for him at Coyote Falls, he must face it alone.

The weather had changed. Instead of the heavy overcast of recent days the sun was shining and sparkled on the wet early morning grass. As he climbed higher the wind freshened and scattered little white clouds about the sky.

He passed the spot where he had found Bingley the first time he had ridden this way. The path grew steeper and even before he entered the trees he could hear the distant roar of the falls. It was louder than previously and as he came in sight of it once again he could see why. The rain and snow in the high peaks had swollen the water courses and now the cascade broke over the rimrock in a solid torrent that leaped far over the ledge and broke on the ears in a deluge of noise.

There was no point in trying to ride the palomino any further and Calhoun slid from the saddle. He hobbled the horse, drew his Winchester and proceeded on foot. He glanced at the sky. The sun was high and he reckoned it was almost noon. His senses were alert because he didn't know what to expect.

He moved up the trail to the edge of

the chasm and looked up at the great curtain of water. Heavy spray flew through the air and one huge rainbow spread across the gorge like an ethereal bridge. He peered over the edge but could see only part of the way down.

Suddenly he felt nervous, as though somebody had come up behind him, and he stepped quickly away. He looked about but there was nobody there. He began to walk towards the falls and when he was halfway to where the trail led behind the torrent he stopped and raised his rifle.

Stepping out from the edge of the falls, partly concealed by spray, was the figure of a man wearing a grimy grey jacket and a peaked cap. Across his arm he carried a rifle. He moved slowly forward with just the suggestion of a limp. Calhoun felt something like fear catch at his throat.

'Carver!' he said. 'I thought you died in the fire!'

As if to confirm his words, as the figure got closer Calhoun could see that his face was blackened and the grey jacket was singed. The blind eye seemed to look beyond him and Calhoun was temped to turn and see what was behind. But with an almost physical effort he continued to move forwards. His nerves were on edge and he still felt that there was something uncanny about the figure approaching him with such slow but unrelenting steps.

Then something clicked in his brain. If his supposition was correct, this was not Carver but the man who had murdered him and taken his identity. It was the man who had betrayed Calhoun and so many others, the man who had been responsible for him spending those ugly months in Andersonville. It was not Carver but Con Reeder who faced him.

'Reeder!' Calhoun called.

The man stopped. They were now quite close. Calhoun could see the scar blazing across Reeder's fire-ravaged cheek and he could see that he had taken him by surprise. The man was nonplussed and that alone would have convinced Calhoun that he was right.

'I know what happened back in Georgia!' Calhoun shouted. 'I know what you did. I know how you betrayed us.'

The man continued to stand immobile. Calhoun had to shout as loud as he could for his voice to be heard above the roar of the falls. Calhoun was about to take another step forward when the man's silence was broken.

'Who the hell are you?' he shouted.

'It's of no concern. All that matters is that I know what happened to Carver.'

There was no sign that the man had registered what Calhoun had said and Calhoun was uncertain whether he had recovered from his initial shock of surprise. The booming of the falls was ringing in his ears with an almost hypnotic effect. Suddenly the stalemate was broken when a voice from the hillside suddenly boomed out.

'No, you don't know what happened to Carver!'

Both men instinctively turned their

faces towards the source of the sound. Standing a little way up the hillside was another man.

'Reeder!' he shouted. 'You thought I was a man called Watts. You imagined I was going to lead you to the treasure. You thought that Carver was long gone.' He broke into a laugh.

'Like my friend says, you're a madman. Welcome to the real world, Reeder.' He turned his attention to Calhoun.

'You got most of it figured!' he shouted, 'but not the last bit. You see, I'm Carver!'

For a moment Calhoun was stunned but then a fog seemed to clear from his brain. Of course, it fitted — even down to the Walker the man he had thought was a government agent had pressed into his hand. Before he could react, however, Reeder suddenly sprang into life. Quickly raising his rifle to his shoulder, he fired at Calhoun and then began to run back down the trail. The shot went winging over Calhoun's head and the next instant he was running down the track in pursuit.

The man was hampered by his slight limp and Calhoun felt that he was gaining on him when he vanished behind the curtain of the falls. Calhoun's blood was up and he pitched forward into the darkness, not considering the danger of Reeder waiting to fire another shot. The path was slippery under foot and he slid sideways as Reeder's rifle barked again. His leg hurt but the slip had saved his life. He picked himself up, and continued in pursuit of Reeder, whose shadowy form he could just make out in the gloom.

As Calhoun emerged into the twilight zone of sunshine and shadow where the trail emerged from behind the falls he was suddenly hit by something heavy. For a moment he didn't know what it was, then came the sickening realization that it was Reeder who, in his desperation, had waited to hurl himself upon Calhoun. For a moment they swayed on the edge of the gulf. Then, with a feeling of cold dread, Calhoun realized that they were going over into the abyss below. For a brief moment he had a glimpse of Reeder's burnt and agonized face twisted into a convulsion of utter fear and rage. His one good eye was blazing with hatred and the livid scar down his cheek stood out like a brand.

Then he was falling though an infinity of space, his arms whirling as he sought desperately for he didn't know what. Above him a thin thread of blue sky was swallowed in the darkness of the gorge and he seemed to fall for a long, long time before, with a tremendous crash which drove all the air from his lungs, he hit the water in the pool below.

The shock of the impact was like hitting something solid. He felt himself going down and down, drawn into the depths of the seething pool by the enormous force of water falling from above and the pressure of the suction below. There was nothing but pandemonium and chaos. Calhoun felt himself tumbling over and over and then for a moment everything was black.

Coming to, he instinctively attempted to rise again but he was pushed under as if by some mighty hand. He could not breathe, could not tell whether he was upside down or right way up. The cascading tide filled his mouth and his nostrils as he struggled to free himself from the weight of waters which held him down. He was fighting to stay alive. Frantically he tried to move his arms, to orientate himself.

Then suddenly the iron clasp which held him loosened its grasp for a moment and he began to climb slowly, laboriously up a steep-sided mountain of suffocation and night. His lungs were bursting. He felt shaken, battered and helpless, but he clung on and wouldn't give up this terrible painful ascent. Up, up, and then there was light on his face, a roaring in his ears and he broke through to the surface.

The waterfall hurled itself over the cliffs high above him but had flung him to one side so that he was in calmer waters, though the seething turbulence was all around him. He gasped for breath, trying to force the air back into his lungs, coughing and spluttering, striving to achieve full consciousness.

Then, inconsequentially, thoughts of Mary flooded like the waters themselves into his brain. He began to flail. He was unsure in what direction he should look for safety, tried to raise his head to get his bearings and see what might be around him. He began to move his arms in a more purposeful way and made a mighty effort to swim towards what he took to be the nearest shore.

He had an impression of trees hanging over the water but they seemed a long way off. He was so exhausted and the water seemed to suck him down. He was confused and deafened by the continuous thunder of the falls above him but slowly he began to move in the direction he wanted. Every stroke was an effort that called for all the supplies of grit and energy he possessed, but he wasn't going to give way now.

There were rocks rearing out of the water. He tried to grasp one but it was too steep and the sides were too slippery. His strength seemed to give way. It was no use. He would never make it after all. But he floundered on, his last reserves of strength almost used up.

There were more rocks. He struggled to reach them. Finding a lower, flatter rock he struggled to climb on to it. He slipped, was pulled back, made a last despairing effort and was almost out of the water when his strength gave way and he was swept away again on the boiling waters.

All he could do was try to keep his head above the surface as the torrent swept him on. He felt an enormous fatigue and his body was racked with pain but he steeled his will to hang on till at last, as he gave a last despairing look at the sky above, which seemed to have expanded in order to enfold him, a kind of darkness descended.

When he came to he saw that he had travelled some distance from the falls, although the noise of their waters still reverberated in his ears. The sound seemed to take on an almost human tone and then, as full consciousness returned, he realized that it wasn't the noise of the falls he could hear but that it was indeed a voice calling loudly to him. He raised himself with difficulty on to one elbow. He seemed to be wedged into some dense tangle of vegetable matter that the river had washed against a narrow strip of shore and coming towards him over some rocks was a figure carrying a rope.

'Mary!' Calhoun breathed.

The figure reached him and he felt a strong grip under his arms pulling him out of the water.

'Mary!' he repeated.

They were on dry land now and he lay gasping in the arms of his rescuer. Calhoun looked up. He didn't recognize the face that looked down on him but then some old memory started to flicker.

'Just take it easy,' the man said. 'Don't try to do too much. It was the snag that saved you.'

'What happened?' Calhoun began. 'How long . . . ?'

'Quite a time. Took me long enough to find a way down here. And I doubt whether there's much left of Reeder.'

Calhoun lay back, waiting for his faculties to return.

'By the way,' the man said, 'sorry to disappoint you. You've probably gathered by now that I ain't Mary. Name's Carver. It's been a long time. Real pleased to meet with you again.'

★ ★ ★

It was a busy morning in Coyote Falls. Calhoun and Mary had just left the café and were crossing the street towards a new building which had gone up where the saloon used to stand.

'Do you really think Norah will be OK?' Calhoun said.

'You worry too much. Of course she'll be OK. She helped run the general store up in Elk Creek, didn't she?'

'That was a long time ago. You've got to admit she's more than a little . . . ' He paused, searching for the right word.

'Eccentric?' Mary suggested, then laughed. 'About as eccentric as a man keeping a cougar for a pet.'

Calhoun glanced down at her, then drew her to him.

'She knows how to cook and she's really taken to the place. She'll cope just fine.'

'Talkin' about copin',' he said. 'Do you reckon you'll be able to handle the two of us together, Cherokee and me?'

'I'm willin' to give it a try.'

They came round a corner on to the main street. Outside a new building where the saloon used to be a buckboard was drawn up. As they approached the door of the building was thrown open and Hiram Bingley appeared.

'Why howdy!' Calhoun called. 'What's your business in town? Need a hand?'

Hiram's face was wreathed in smiles.

'Just about finished here,' he said. 'Movin' right in. You can help me hang this up if you like.'

He reached into the buckboard, pulled out a large wooden sign and held it up for them to read:

Hiram J. Bingley. Attorney at Law.

'That's fine,' Mary said. 'So you've found your new premises?'

'Sure have. Couldn't be better. Right here on Main Street and I'll be livin' right above the office.'

'And just across from my brother,' Mary said. 'Kind of appropriate, if you see what I mean.'

Almost as if he had heard her words, the marshal appeared in his doorway and waved to them across the street.

'You should have let me come with you to the falls,' Bingley said, turning to Calhoun.

'Yeah. Maybe so. I just figured this was somethin' I needed to sort out by myself.'

'I gather you and Mr Carver go back aways?'

'Sure do. Which reminds me, Mr Carver is comin' round tonight. Why don't you join us for supper?' Calhoun looked at Mary as if for confirmation.

'Of course,' she said. 'About seven OK?'

'That's mighty neighbourly of you.'

With a little help from Calhoun and the marshal Bingley's sign was soon swinging from the wall above the boardwalk.

'I like Mr Bingley,' Mary said as they walked away. 'He'll be good to have around.'

'He'll be more than good,' Calhoun replied, thinking over all that had happened recently. 'Mr Hiram J. Bingley is the man for Coyote Falls. He is the future of the West.'

THE END

We do hope that you have enjoyed reading this large print book.

Did you know that all of our titles are available for purchase?

We publish a wide range of high quality large print books including:
Romances, Mysteries, Classics
General Fiction
Non Fiction and Westerns

Special interest titles available in large print are:
The Little Oxford Dictionary
Music Book, Song Book
Hymn Book, Service Book

Also available from us courtesy of Oxford University Press:
Young Readers' Dictionary
(large print edition)
Young Readers' Thesaurus
(large print edition)

For further information or a free brochure, please contact us at:
Ulverscroft Large Print Books Ltd.,
The Green, Bradgate Road, Anstey,
Leicester, LE7 7FU, England.
Tel: (00 44) **0116 236 4325**
Fax: (00 44) **0116 234 0205**

IRON EYES IS DEAD

Rory Black

Desert Springs was an oasis that drew the dregs of Texas down into its profitable boundaries. Among the many ruthless characters, there was none so fearsome as the infamous bounty hunter, Iron Eyes. He had trailed a dangerous outlaw right into the remote settlement. But Iron Eyes was wounded: shot up with arrow and bullet after battling with a band of Apaches. As the doctor fought to save him, was the call true that Iron Eyes was dead?

TAKE THE OREGON TRAIL

Eugene Clifton

Thousands of men had taken the trail to the west looking for a new beginning — many didn't make it. Adam Trant had also set out on the Oregon Trail — but he was looking for an old enemy. The hunt took him to a savage wilderness and matched him against deadly marauders. Adam was ready to die, as long as he succeeded in his quest. However, he wasn't ready for the unpredictable force of the love of a woman.

FOOL'S PLAY

Carl Williams

Royce rides into Jawbone looking for a doctor, but finds trouble. Living by the gun can he expect anything else? He signs on with land baron Yale Jamerson, hoping for a job that will leave his conscience clear. However, when Jamerson plans to dam the river and charge road tolls, the townspeople revolt. Forced to choose between his livelihood and his conscience, Royce must decide which path to take. Will it lead to a showdown with his closest friend?

THE VENOM OF VALKO

Michael D. George

The bounty for the capture of the Valko Kid is a fortune, drawing the lowest of the low to try and claim it. On one bright moonlit night, Sheriff Colby Masters leads his posse to a narrow canyon ridge to await Valko, who is heading for the town of War Smoke. Suddenly below them, thundering through the canyon, rides a horseman clad in black and riding a magnificent white stallion . . . Soon they will all taste *The Venom of Valko* . . .